B, MY N

—— Bunny

Look for these other books
about best friends
by NORMA FOX MAZER:

A, My Name Is Ami
C, My Name Is Cal
D, My Name Is Danita
E, My Name Is Emily

B, MY NAME IS
Bunny

NORMA FOX MAZER

AN
APPLE
PAPERBACK

SCHOLASTIC INC.
New York Toronto London Auckland Sydney

ISBN 0-590-43895-6

13 12 11 10 9 8 7 6 5 4 3 2   4   4 5 6 7 8 9/9

Printed in the U.S.A.   40

*This one is for my mother,
Jean Garlen Fox*

Chapter 1

I might as well tell you my name and get it over with. Are you ready for this? Bunny. No, that's not a nickname. That is my whole, real, entire birth name. B-U-N-N-Y. Okay, time out for the yuk-yuks and the bunny jokes, as in Easter bunnies, bunny rabbits, hippitty hoppitty, bunny fur, cuddle bunny, and dumb bunny. And, definitely, let's not forget Bugs Bunny.

The year we were in fifth grade, every time Davis Buck saw me (which was about twenty-five times a day), he'd say, "What's up, Doc?" And he'd shove his front teeth out — rabbit teeth, get it? Then he'd say, "Geeeeze, guys, I godda eat my ledduce."

What did I do? Acted like I could care less. My best friend, Emily Boots, and I figured out that was the way to drive Davis Buck crazy. I really hated him that year, but, in some ways, like I told Emily, how could you blame Davis? I got stuck with a silly name.

Don't try to tell that to my mother. "But, sweetie, Bunny is an old family name. You know I named you for my Aunt Bunny."

Maybe. And maybe Mom was in her animal phase when I was born. The way she was in her nature phase for my brother and her cosmic phase for my sister. Still, Shad and Star definitely got the better deal. Shad is not such a bad name for a boy, as long as you don't know it's short for Shadbush, which is my mother's favorite spring tree. My sister's name is Starship Larrabee. Not a great name to be stuck with, but it does shorten down nicely to Star.

I wouldn't mind being called a name that has to do with the universe. Though, come to think of it, after Star, what is there? Globe? Planet? Meteor? I guess I ought to be glad my mom wasn't still out in space when I was born.

That's when she and Dad bought our house. Star was five years old then. My mother says the first word I learned to say was "Mama" and the second word was "mine." She says I used to walk around our house, patting the walls and saying, "Mine, mine, mine."

Dad calls our house the old monster. It has ten rooms, three chimneys, and four fireplaces, but only one works. Our plumbing gets into trouble about twice a year. Mom says we should replace the roof. My father says we can live with that for a while longer, but the hot water tank is shot.

My room has a slanted ceiling, a window seat, and old wallpaper with faded yellow roses. My father said I could have the room redone as a birthday present, but I said, No, thanks!

Emily lives in an apartment and her mother is always worrying about upsetting the landlord, who lives downstairs. Emily envies me our house, but it evens out because I envy her her name. I think Emily is the perfect name. It's pretty, it's old-fashioned, and for extra measure, it's the name of a famous poet, Emily Dickinson. Emily's mother likes poetry.

My mom says I shouldn't let my name make me unhappy. She should talk. At least once a week she brings up how sorry she is that she didn't keep her own last name when she married Dad.

Before Mom was Lorraine Larrabee, she was Lorraine Watjoichkas. That looks harder to say than it is. All you have to do is say, Watch Your Kiss, but you have to say it fast. Wachyerkiss. I learned how to say that a long time before I knew how it was spelled. Watch-Your-Kiss made perfect sense to me, because my Grandma Watjoichkas was always kissing me when she came to visit.

Grandma lives in Toronto. I usually get to visit her — alone — at least once a year. Even though her hair is totally white, she's not at all the person you would expect from just thinking of the word "grandmother." She's very slim and wears jeans, big dangly silver earrings, and really bright silk blouses. She says, "I have to live my life, not according to any predetermined idea, but as to how I feel." What this means is that my grandmother will always surprise you.

This year I grew taller than both my grandmother and my sister. One more inch and I'll be looking down on my mother and creeping right up there on my father. Mom says, "There must have been some very tall genes somewhere back there in our family."

"Just call me the family freak," I say.

Which makes my father give me a nervous look. Is my daughter revving up to be a candidate for therapy? But after a moment, I can see by the way his eyebrows relax that he's decided I'm too normal to be abnormal.

In our class at school, I'm the tallest girl and nearly the tallest person. There is one other girl who's almost as tall as me, Ami Pelter, but it's different for her. First, on a person like Ami, being tall looks good. She's really cute! Second, she doesn't have buck teeth (I do, which is another reason Davis's making rabbit teeth at me drove me completely crazy), and third, if Ami did have buck teeth, I *know* her father would get them fixed. I have Mr. Pelter for language arts, and I can tell you, he's that kind of sympathetic person who would take another person's problems seriously.

Not my father. He says, "You don't have an overbite, Bunny. It's all in your mind." He would say that. He's a psychologist.

"Dad, I've got news for you. These teeth are not in my mind. They are in my *mouth*."

"Your teeth give you character," my mother says. For once, she agrees with Dad. I know why. They don't want to spend the money. Sure, braces are big bucks, but it's my mouth and my teeth.

I told Emily, "I'm doomed to go around forever with crooked teeth."

"Bunny, really, your teeth don't stick out." Em-

4

ily has a way of frowning and looking me over with her head tipped to one side. "They're not completely straight. But it's not noticeable to anybody."

Even though I still think they stick out, I feel better when Emily says that. At least, until the next time I look in the mirror.

Emily also doesn't think I'm too tall. About that, all she will say is, "Bunny! How can a person be too tall?"

To which I say, "Emily, if you were as tall as me, *you'd know*."

Last year, in sixth grade, our school played Durwin Middle School for the citywide basketball championship. The next morning, when I took the paper in, there we were, right on the sports page. And there *I* was, jumping in the air for the basket, and looking huge. Underneath, it said: *Despite the efforts of Bunny (Toooo Tall) Larrabee for her team, Drumlins Middle School lost to Durwin 55–76.*

Next day in school: "How's Bunny 'Toooo Tall' Larrabee this morning?" And that wasn't even a kid! It was Mr. Maxwell, our homeroom teacher. What a tease. I feel sorry for his kids.

Some people think, because of my father's work, being a psychologist, he must be the ideal, understanding father figure. News flash! My dad is fat — well, overweight — and he smokes too much, and he really knows how to bug me. For instance, he gets SO anxious about me if I'm out two seconds after 9 P.M. What does he think is going to happen? I'll look at a boy and turn into green cheese? Or maybe the werewolves come out then.

Shad is four years younger than me, but already

Dad doesn't fuss much if he comes in from playing *later* than me. This is one case where I'm really glad my mother disagrees with him. "Bill, you are not going to limit Bunny that way. Now, if you're worried about your daughter, you get out there and do something about the people you're *really* worried about. Which is, let's face it, other males."

Mom works for the police department. She's not a cop. She's definitely not the type to arrest anyone. She's an artist, and she works in public relations.

She and Officer Friendly are a team. Every day, they visit hospitals and schools and while Officer Friendly is telling the kids about safety rules, my mom is drawing pictures. Sometimes she draws the kids and gives them their pictures afterward, sometimes she uses the overhead projector and draws pictures to illustrate what Officer Friendly is saying.

Since my father is a psychologist, he and Mom are sort of in the same business — helping people. But that doesn't mean they get along like peanut butter and jelly. When they disagree, they call it "having a discussion." When Shad and I do the same thing, it's a fight. Shad usually wins our arguments. He's sort of relentless.

I don't know who wins when Mom and Dad go at it, but Dad has an advantage, like Mom says, in any argument — excuse me! *discussion* — because of being a psychologist. He can always rip out some big word describing your personality, or your emotional tendencies, or your character flaws. Not that he does, very much. He's really sort of a gentle person.

His favorite thing to talk about, actually, is Multiple Personality Ripples, which is his own discovery. He's going to write a book about it someday. People with MPR are basically normal, but (my father says) they don't have a really fixed personality. Their personalities bop around, so they're one way one time and another way another time.

Now this could be a description of my mom. Last night, I was in the bathroom washing my hair over the tub, and she came in to brush her teeth. "Did you rinse all the soap out?" she said, and she turned on the shower.

"Mom!" I screamed. "Cold water! That's sadistic."

"You have to get all the soap out, honey."

"I'm doing it. I'm doing it!" I stood up and wrapped my head in a towel.

She started toweling my hair dry. "You have such pretty hair, Bunny. It's so thick and healthy."

See what I mean about MPR? Now she was being really nice. I leaned against her, and I don't know how it happened but we got to talking about my problems, such as my teeth, my height, Dad's attitude about makeup, and etcetera.

Mom listened for a while, then she said, "Look, Bunny, I want to tell you something. There's no use moaning about your problems."

I straightened up. "I'm not moaning."

"Well, chewing them over, or whatever you're doing. I don't even think most of them are problems, but since you do, why not think of them like a bunch of bananas. You don't try to rip off all the bananas at one go, do you?" She started brushing her teeth, which was what she originally came in for.

Bunny: "But, Mom — "

Mom (with a mouth full of foam): "You take one banana at a time, right? It's the same with whatever bothers you. You have six problems? Same as having six bananas. Take one off. You have five left."

"Mom, that's a really neat comparison, but bananas get ripe, then they get rotten."

"My point exactly! So do problems if you don't attack them."

"But when bananas get rotten, you throw them out."

Mom (rinsing her mouth): "Same with problems. Think of them like bananas. Visualize them! Imagine you're throwing them out."

"Okay, I'm throwing out bananas." I started pitching imaginary bananas over my head. "Oh, Mom, sorry, that one splatted on the wall!"

"Sweetie! Everything with you is a joke. This visualization might really work." She went off to find my father and see what he thought about it. I went downstairs and phoned Emily.

Chapter 2

I like to make people laugh. I might be a comedian, someday, someone like Phyllis Diller or Joan Rivers. I don't know if I can, but I think about it. I get in a certain mood and I can't be serious about anything. I crack jokes or make remarks, which I HOPE are funny. Sometimes I do this, even when I don't want to.

And then sometimes — not too often, I admit — I'm totally serious. I don't want to tell any jokes. I don't want to hear any jokes. I might just lie on my bed and listen to music and think about things. When Emily's parents got divorced last year, I was like that. Emily and I were both sad for a long time. And even after weeks had passed and I didn't think about what happened to her so much, I couldn't stop thinking about how lucky I was to have my parents and my family.

But my main personality is to be lighthearted

and have a good time. I like trying out my jokes and practicing routines in my room. I haven't gone public yet. So far the person I most make laugh is Emily. She's really easy. I'll give you an example.

Yesterday, she asked me if I noticed the new guy in math class.

Bunny: "What new guy?"

Emily: "You didn't see that new guy? He was sitting right across from you."

Bunny: "I didn't see anyone. . . ." Pause. "Unless you mean the guy with the wave in his hair? Was wearing a green shirt with white stripes? Mickey Mouse watch on his left arm? Had tiny ears? Dirt smudge on his right cheek?"

I was ready to go on, but Emily was laughing too hard to hear anything, anyway.

One trouble with being a funny person is that sometimes people don't know when you're being serious. You'd think my father, being a psychologist, could tell the difference, wouldn't you? Last night, after supper, he asked me to help him clip the privet hedge in front of our house. What he really wanted was to get me without my mother around, so he could lecture me about growing up too fast.

"Bunny. I know you are basically a sensible girl, but sometimes you — I mean, not necessarily YOU, but someone with another person — can get carried away and do things that are not necessarily in that first person's — OR the second person's — best interest. Do you follow me?"

Sure I did. I've had all my life to figure out what my father is talking about when he gets going on a subject. 1. Growing up too fast means I wore eye shadow to school. 2. "Someone" refers to me. 3. The "other person" has to be Emily. As to getting carried away, my question is, Where?

Maybe he worries because I am sort of impulsive, but I don't think I'm a dope. And I know Emily isn't! I've even heard my mother say, "For a girl her age, she has both feet on the ground."

"Are you listening to me?" my father said.

"Sure, Dad."

"What I'm saying is not for your amusement."

Was I smiling? I put on a stern expression. "Sorry, Dad!"

"I'm trying to have a talk here with you, Bunny."

"Yes, Dad!"

"Okay, okay, listen to what I'm saying. I don't think makeup is appropriate for your age — and while I'm at it, I don't want you to get involved with dating for a very long time."

Did he really have to say it? Emily and I have talked about dating and boys and all that stuff, and we've decided we're never going to act desperate, like some girls do. *Ohh, ohhh, I don't have a boyfriend. What will I do? Who will I go to the movies with? There's a party coming! I don't have a date!*

We think this is really stupid. What's wrong with going to the movies with your girl friend? Do you have to have a date for a party? If Emily and I go to a party together, we just have a lot of fun. And we don't think it's the end of the world if we dance with each other.

A lot of girls feel like they have to have a boyfriend for status, or something. Their life isn't complete without a boyfriend. It's not like they fall in love. Mari Champion, who's the biggest flirt in our class, is *always* falling in love. So she says. I say, Gimme a break! At our age, you don't fall in love. I mean, everybody knows that. Emily and I agree that really falling in love is different.

We talk about all this stuff, we talk about everything. There's nobody else I can talk to like Emily.

But even Emily reads me wrong sometimes. Today we were in the cafeteria, eating lunch, and I happened to ask her what her mother's real name was. Right away, she wanted to know what was the joke.

"No joke. What's your mother's real name?"

"You know. Ann Boots."

"I said her real name."

"Is it a riddle?"

"Emily, this is a question in the spirit of curiosity. Scholarship can't flourish without curiosity," I said, quoting my father. And I threw in a little nose snort, the way he does.

Emily giggled.

"Thank you," I said. "Now, don't you know what your mama's name was before she married your papa?"

"Oh! That! Why didn't you say so? Her name was Simpson."

"Well, that's a perfectly lovely name. Why did she change it to Boots?"

"Bunny, she got married!"

"She didn't have to marry your father's name. She only had to marry him."

"Bunny, when you get married — "

"IF I get married."

" — you can keep your name."

"That's when I throw my name away, Emily.

Good-bye, Bunny! But, I'll keep Larrabee."

"Well, when I get married, I'm going to take my husband's name."

"No! That's so unliberated."

"Bunny, you can do things your way. I'll do things my way!"

Mom says the way Emily and I bicker, we are like an old married couple. One thing I know, we'll never get a divorce. We are friends for life. I can't even imagine life without Emily. It's like trying to imagine life without my mom.

Chapter 3

"Hello, who's this?"

"This is Bunny. Is this Christopher? Is Emily there?"

"This isn't Christopher. It's Wilma."

"Sorry, Wilma, I thought you were Chris. Will you get Emily for me?"

"Who?"

"Your sister."

"Who's this?"

"Who do you think it is, Wilma? I just told you. It's me, Bunny."

"This isn't Wilma, this is Christopher."

"Wilma!"

"Don't call me Wilma. That's not my name. Who is this? Why do you sound so unfriendly? I don't think this is Bunny."

"Take my word for it, this is Bunny Larrabee. Who is this, Wilma or Christopher?"

Silence.

"Christopher? Wilma? Whichever one you are, will you get your sister? I'm asking you nicely. Will you please call Emily to the phone?"

Silence.

"Christopher."

Silence.

"Wilma."

Silence.

I drummed my fingers on the table. I whistled. I hummed. I thought I could outwait whichever Boots twin it was. My guess, Wilma. She was always up to something. Chris was mostly her follower.

"Wilma, want to hear a stupid joke? There are these two girls and their names are Fort and Snort."

I thought I heard a little giggle. "Snort ate Fort's strawberry pie. Fort got mad and said, 'Snort! You are the dumbest, most selfish, stingiest, greediest person in the world!' 'Well, SAME TO YOU,' said Snort. 'Oh,' said Fort, 'what a low-down thing to say to your best friend!' "

I waited. Not even a snicker. "You're right, it's a crummy joke. But don't blame me, I got it off a bubble gum wrapper. Now will you get Emily. PLEASE!"

"Don't yell! You're hurting my ears."

"You know what, Chris Boots? Or Wilma Boots? Or whoever you are? If you don't get Emily right away, and I mean pronto, I'm going to come over there and haunt you."

BANG! Down went the phone. She — or he — hung up on me. Poor Emily! She always gets stuck taking care of the twins. Her mom is a nurse, and her father lives in Chicago with his other family. I guess Mrs. Boots doesn't have a lot of money and can't afford baby-sitters too often.

Sometimes I feel guilty thinking about how much Emily has to do and how I don't have to do half as much. Sure, I take care of Shad, but he's nine and that makes a big difference. He doesn't even like the idea that I'm baby-sitting him.

I waited a couple of minutes, then I dialed again. This time when the phone rang, Emily picked it up. "Who answered the phone before?" I said. "Was that Chris or Wilma?"

"Wilma. Was that you calling? What'd you say to her, Bunny? She was yelling, 'Don't let her! Don't let her!' What'd you tell her you were going to do?"

"Haunt her."

"Bunny! That's mean."

"Em-ily, you don't even know what happened. I was provoked. She wouldn't get you, just hung on the line, breathing. You know I like Wilma, but she can be a real brat sometimes."

Emily didn't say anything for a moment. Then, very quietly, she said, "Well, don't you think it was kind of bratty of you to scare her, Bunny?"

I hate it when Emily gets that quiet, quiet voice. It always makes me feel stupid and in the wrong. "It was just a little joke."

"Not a very funny one."

"How did I know she was going to get spooked?"

"She's only a little kid." Emily still had her quiet voice.

I started to feel really punk. I was mad, and my thoughts were mean thoughts. Emily was so righteous. I couldn't even make a small mistake without her getting on my case. What would she say if Wilma hit me over the head with a shovel? There'd be blood dripping down my face and Emily would say in her quiet voice, "Well, Bunny, we have to understand that she's just a curious child."

One of my Personality Ripples is a tendency to act first and think later. I said, "If that's the way you feel, why don't we just forget it!" And I did to Emily what Wilma had done to me — hung up on her.

The phone rang again about two minutes later. I was sure it was Emily. I let it ring three times before I picked it up. "Hello, Emily," I said, "do you have something to tell me?"

"Bun?" It was my sister.

"Star! Hi! Where are you? You sound like you're right across the street. Are you here?"

"No, I'm in Rhode Island. What would I be doing there? Is Mom home? I want to talk to her."

"Star, what are you doing? I mean, how's school? Are you doing a lot of painting?" When Star graduated high school she got a medal for being the best all-around artist.

"Everything's okay," she said. "Is Mom around? Will you get her for me?"

She didn't ask me anything, not one thing about myself. On top of Emily, that was too much. I called Mom to the phone, then I went into the kitchen and attacked a carton of Heavenly Hash. Here's where it's a real drag to have a father who's a psychologist. I can't pig out without G-U-I-L-T, because I know what Dad thinks of eating to make yourself feel better. With every delicious spoonful,

I could hear his grave voice in my head, *"Sublimating your negative feelings with food. . . . Using food as a substitute for affection. . . ."*

I pretty much demolished the carton. Suddenly, just as I gulped down the last ice-cold spoonful, I got this really vicious throbbing over my right eye. Maybe I had a brain tumor. They'd have to operate, open up my skull, dig out the tumor with sharp knives. With my luck, the operation would be a failure. Sudden death on the operating table. Or maybe I'd live, but my mind would be affected permanently. My brains would be scrambled, my memory gone. I could see myself in the hospital, my head covered in a white bandage. I was all alone. Oh, of course Mom and Dad would come to see me — Shad, too — but no one else.

Shad came into the kitchen. "What're you eating?"

Ordinarily, I wouldn't even answer an obvious question like that. But since Shad was visiting me in the hospital when I was on my death bed, I felt kindly disposed toward him. "I'm sorry, there's hardly any left. Here." I held out the carton. "Take the rest."

He looked in the carton. "The rest of what?"

"Shad," I said in my sweetest voice, "had I known you desired some Heavenly Hash, believe me, I would have left you a large portion."

Shad pushed his glasses back on his nose. "Did you and Emily fight again?"

"What kind of question is that?"

"What'd you fight about this time?"

"Shut up, please. It's none of your business."

"Make me some cinnamon toast."

"Why?"

"Because you didn't leave me any ice cream."

"That doesn't make sense, Shad!"

"It does to me." He sat down at the table. "I'll explain it to you, Bunny. See, there are some things in the house that just belong to one person, like my animals belong to me. And there are some things that don't belong to just one person, like tv and ice cream. And when someone hogs them — "

See what I mean about being relentless? I know Shad. He would sit right there and talk the ears off me until I did what he wanted. I made cinnamon toast.

I went up to my room, but I didn't feel like doing homework. I was just thinking about Emily. When you've been friends as long as Emily and I have been, it makes you feel really strange to not be friends, even for an hour.

I decided to call her. I wasn't going to be *humble*, but if she wanted to make up, I would, too. I picked up the phone. Mom and Star were still on! I heard Star saying, "But, Mom, I don't fit into — Is somebody on? I heard a click."

"It's me," I said. "I just wanted to see if the phone was free."

"It's not, so please get off. Mom and I are still talking."

"Well, excuse me, my beloved older sister. Pardon me for taking up your precious time."

"Bunny, what's your problem? I can't talk to you right now."

"Don't give it a thought. I know you won't." I hung up.

Later, when I called Emily, she said she'd been

trying to call me, but our phone was busy every time. "I guess you were right about Wilma," she said.

"No, you're right, she's a little kid. I shouldn't have teased her."

"Mom left me a note, saying I should make tuna cheese casserole for supper," Emily said. "I must have used the wrong cheese. It was one of those strong cheeses. You know what Wilma said when she tasted it?"

"Let me guess. She said, 'This casserole tastes like dirty socks! And I ain't eating it.'"

"I hate to tell you how close you are," Emily said.

Chapter 4

On Thursdays, Emily doesn't have to go straight home. The twins have swimming practice. So we always go to my house. I knocked on Shad's door. I'm supposed to check up that he's okay. "What're you doing?"

He opened the door. He had a white rat on each shoulder.

"I'll be in my room if you want anything, Shad."

"Hi, Shad," Emily said.

He petted his rats and didn't say anything. Emily and I went to my room. "Is he mad at me or something?" she asked.

"No. I think he likes you."

"Well, I didn't think he hated me."

"No, I mean, he *likes* you."

"Oh!" She blushed.

That's typical of Emily. I mean, most girls our age wouldn't blush if a nine-year-old boy had a crush on them. A lot of boys, not just Shad, like Emily. She doesn't even realize it. She doesn't even know how pretty she is. She has long dark hair, brown eyes, and freckles across her cheeks. And she has an excellent personality, except that she doesn't have a lot of self-confidence. Sometimes I'm very sympathetic about it and try to build her up. But sometimes, I just get annoyed.

We sat down on my bed and showed each other our books. It's something we do all the time. She gave me her book first. "As soon as you get done reading it, give it back, because I'm going to read it again."

I looked at the cover. It showed this cute girl in a swimming pool. And a very cute boy, sitting at a table under an awning and looking at her. They were both in swimsuits. I read the back of the book, then I looked inside and then at the author's name. "Oh, I know her! Didn't she write — "

"Uh huh, the story about the boy who was so — "

" — mixed up," I said. Emily nodded. We do that sometimes. We finish each other's sentences.

"Wait till you read it," she said. "This is a great book."

Then I showed her my book. I think we started this in fourth grade. It was Emily's idea. She really likes reading more than I do.

"Is this good?" Emily said.

"Very good book," I said. "Funny. But never mind that. Look at the cover. Don't you want to die?"

On the cover was a picture of a guy. You didn't see all of him. You didn't have to! Just his face was enough. He had thick, wavy dark hair; incredible eyelashes; and a look in his eyes that made you want to drop dead on the spot.

"Wouldn't you like to meet him?" I said.

"What if you did? What would you say?" Emily brought the book right up to her nose. She's near-sighted. "I thought maybe they'd have his name on the cover."

"I'm going to write to the author," I said, "and ask for his name."

"No, you're not."

"I am."

She laughed and put the book in her purse. I don't think she believed me. "Bunny, Mom and I were talking about the twins' birthday party, and I had this idea about you."

"What idea?"

"I probably shouldn't tell you. You won't like it."

"What is it?"

She rolled over on the bed. "No, now that I think about it, it's probably a really dumb idea. Just forget I said anything."

"Emily! Tell me what your idea is." This was one of those times when her low self-esteem was really annoying.

"I thought maybe you could be — this is kind of a goofy idea, Bunny, but what if you dressed up as a clown and — "

"You mean, be a clown for the twins' party?"

"It's stupid, isn't it?"

"I like that, Em. That's a good idea."

"It is?"

"Yes. It sounds like fun."

"You'd really like to do it?"

"It'll be a blast. I've got to get a good costume."

"You could wear bunny ears."

"No! What a stupid idea."

Her face got red again, and she looked sort of miserable. I always feel like a huge, gross beast when I hurt her feelings, but she ought to know how I feel about bunny jokes by this time.

"You said a clown. Maybe I'll do baggy pants. What else?"

"A wig?" Emily said.

"Does your mother have one?"

"No! Why would you say that, Bunny? My mother's not bald."

We stared at each other. Were we fighting? I fanned my hands out behind my ears and crossed my eyes. No reason. Just a funny face. Emily started laughing, so that was okay again.

"What about whiteface makeup?" I said. "Where can I get that?"

"On Richmond Street, there's a theatrical store, they sell costumes and stuff. I bet they'll have it."

That's just the way Emily is. She knows a lot of things, and it's rare when she doesn't have good ideas.

April 10

Dear Mr. Diment,

My name is Bunny Larrabee. I'm 13 years old and in the seventh grade in Drumlins Middle School. I like to read, ski, skate, cook (somewhat), swim, and (you may think this is sort of strange), I also REALLY like to make people laugh. In fact, someday, I hope to be a famous comedy star.

Well, the reason I wrote is that I just read your book, Paris Plus, and it's very good. On a scale of one to ten, I would definitely rate it as a nine and a half. One of the things I liked about your book is that there were jokes and other humerous remarks in it.

Another thing I was most interested in was the main character. Where did you ever get the name Paris? That's a pretty strange name. But even with that name, Paris was somebody I would like to meet. He was a very sensitive and interesting person. One of the things I liked about Paris was the way he would only wear white tennies, even when he went to a formal dance! I recommended this book to my girl friend.

I congratulate you on your great talent in writing. I hope you continue to write such good books. I do have one question to ask you. Could you please send me the name and address of the guy on the cover? I'd also like his telephone number and the date of his birthday. He looks very interesting, just the way Paris should look, and I think it might be fun to be pen pals with him. I hope this is not too much trouble for you!

Sincerely, A Lifetime Fan,

B. Larrabee

Chapter 5

The first thing Emily and I noticed when we got together in the cafeteria for lunch was that we were both wearing red shirts and dark blue pants. This kind of thing happens to us all the time. We wear the same kind of clothes or the same colors, without ever checking with each other.

We sat down. I was so hungry I wolfed down my food in record seconds, while Emily was still working on the first half of her sandwich. "Anything you don't want to eat," I said, "pass this way." I leaned close and talked in her ear. The cafeteria is a zoo at lunchtime. "I've been working on my clown routine."

Emily nodded. She didn't say anything, just nibbled at her sandwich.

I should have noticed that she seemed extra quiet, but I didn't. I told her about the letter I wrote to Mr. Diment. "Do you think he'll write back to me?"

"Mr. Diment, or the guy on the cover?"

"Either one! When I get Paris's address, I'm going to write to him. I'll send him my gorgeous picture. No, I better not do that. I'll send him your gorgeous picture."

"I wouldn't have the nerve to write him."

"We'll write him together. We'll tell him we're his fans and admirers. We'll tell him his eyes are dark, mysterious pools and his lips are beautiful fruit. We'll write to him that his teeth are like pearly shells and his eyelashes alone drive us crazy. Emily, how will we sign our letter to our hero?"

She shrugged and half smiled.

"We could be mysterious and just sign our initials," I said. "E. and B. Let him guess. Or maybe our last names. Larrabee and Boots. I like that. It has a ring to it. Do you like it?"

Emily didn't answer. I snapped my fingers in her face. "Hello, in there. Don't mind me. I love talking to myself."

Emily frowned. "Sorry, Bunny. I was thinking — "

"Is *that* what you call it?" Just another funny, or not so funny, remark. I didn't mean anything by it. But Emily flushed, her freckles suddenly stood out all over her face, and she got up and took her tray over to the trash bin.

I went after her. I couldn't figure out why, all of a sudden, Emily was mad at me. "What's the matter?" I said. "Why are you mad?"

She pushed past me toward the door. "I'm not mad, Bunny."

"Well, you're doing a pretty good imitation. What did I do?"

She looked me right in the face. "Nothing, Bunny. You didn't do anything. You're just being yourself. Joke, joke, joke. Ha, ha, ha. Everything is so funny."

"Oh, I see. You didn't like my jokes. Wait, I'll tell you a few new ones. Did you hear about the half-size aspirin for people with splitting headaches? Or how about the horse at the racetrack who had an itch? When he came up to the post, guess what? He got scratched."

"There you go again. Everything is a joke. I don't know, maybe it's me. Forget I said anything. It's just that sometimes your joking gets on my nerves. You know, people can have serious things on their minds and they don't want to hear jokes all the time."

My face must have been as red as my shirt. My neck was hot and my hands got damp. We were standing in the doorway. I just stopped myself from giving the wall a good hard kick. "You make me feel so stupid!" I whispered. I walked out of the cafeteria, down the corridor.

"Bunny." Emily was right behind me. "You want to know — "

"I don't want to know anything. Just go away. Just stay away from me, so I don't get on your nerves. Go find somebody serious to be your friend."

"Bunny!"

Ms. Linsley, the science teacher, came toward us. "Hello, girls."

"Hello, Ms. Linsley." We both said it and smiled, as if everything was perfect. We watched her go down the corridor. Neither of us said anything until she was out of earshot.

Then Emily looked at me and shrugged. "I didn't mean to make you mad," she said. "I don't want you to be mad at me."

"I really noticed that, Emily."

"Well, I just lost my temper. Aren't I allowed to lose my temper?"

"Lose it as much as you want. Who cares? I don't!"

"You don't mean that, Bunny."

"Yes, I do. I guess our friendship has gone on too long. You feel you can be mean to me, say anything you want. You know something? I think you enjoy being mean to me."

"No, I don't! I'm not like that." Her eyes got big.

I could tell I had made a direct hit. I was glad. She wasn't the only one whose feelings could be hurt.

"Am I like that?" she said. "I'm mean to you? You sound like you hate me. Can we talk about this, Bunny?"

"Go ahead. Talk. Say anything you want to. You want me to listen? I'll listen. I listen to you when you talk. I don't just go off into my own thoughts, because I don't find you boring! But I can understand that you don't want to hear anything I have to say, because with me it's all jokes. Not serious stuff."

"Will you shut up for a moment," Emily said in her quietest voice, "and *listen*. I'm sorry, Bunny! I just — " She broke off, her lips pressed together, shaking her head. "I don't know — I don't know what got into me. I took it out on you. I have something on my mind — " She broke off again. Her face got a watery look.

I know Emily. She never cries, she holds everything in. Even when her parents told her they were getting a divorce, she didn't cry. If my parents divorced, I know I'd bawl a bucket of tears. But Emily only gets that watery look on her face. And every time, it gets to me. Did I say the first time I ever saw Emily was in kindergarten and she was crying? I sat down next to her and I thought, Well, I just have to take care of her. I don't know why I thought that, but ever since then we've been best friends.

"Emily?" I touched her shoulder.

She bent over the water fountain and took a long drink. "It's my father, he called last night."

We walked down the corridor and went up the stairs. We stopped under the window looking out over the playing field. It's where we like to go to talk.

"Remember he promised that I could visit over spring vacation?" Emily said. "And he was going to pay for my ticket and send Mom money so she could hire a baby-sitter for Wilma and Chris? So I could spend time alone with him and Marcia and the baby?"

"Of course I remember." I was going to Toronto to visit my grandmother at the same time. We had planned to call each other from Toronto and Chicago. "What happened? He's not going to do it? He broke his promises? That's ratty!"

"No, don't say that. You don't know, Bunny." She bit her lip. "He really wants me to come, but he doesn't have the money right now. He explained it all to me. They've got a lot of expenses. Marcia just had a huge dentist bill. And the baby

30

had to have some kind of surgery to correct something about her feet. And then their car broke down, the engine or something."

"So what?" I said. "Does that mean you can't come visit? Why doesn't he borrow the money?"

"He doesn't like to borrow. He doesn't like to be in debt. He says it's hard enough now, with us and Mom. Bunny, sometimes I wish — " She stopped.

"What?"

"It's nothing, just — I know Mom and Dad didn't get along and all that. I'm *glad* they didn't stay together and go on being miserable. I really am. But I miss him. I miss him so much. And I don't think he misses me."

"Oh, Emily. He does. He does miss you!"

Her lips tightened. "If he missed me so much, wouldn't he do something to get me out to visit him? Why did he have to move to Chicago, anyway? Why couldn't he stay right here where he could see me and the twins?"

"You told me yourself that he had a great new job out there. Anyway, Emily, I know your father. He loves you a lot. Remember when he took us both up in the balloon?"

Every year, a town near us, Jamesville, has a Balloon Festival in June. Not the kind of balloon you blow up, but the kind you go around the world in eighty days in. If the weather is good that weekend, you can look up into the sky and see dozens of huge, colored, striped, and flowered balloons floating over the countryside.

Emily always wanted to go up in one, and two years ago, Mr. Boots treated us both to a balloon ride. We loved it from the moment we stepped into the basket. And once we lifted into the air, we were so excited and so awed that we held hands and didn't say a word.

It wasn't anything like being in an airplane. That's like being in a room. In the balloon, you never forget where you are. You're in the air. You're in this big basket in the air. You're floating. You can look down and see people below you, and houses, trees, everything.

We went over a farm. A kid on a tractor looked up and waved. Some birds flew by. "Did you see that? Did you see that?" Mr. Boots said. He was as excited as we were. "I never saw birds so close!" All you could hear was the wind and then the hiss of the burners heating up the air in the balloon.

"I haven't thought of the balloon ride in ages," Emily said. "That was so great."

I rubbed her shoulder. "Are you okay now?"

She nodded.

"If you're still sad, I could tell you another joke. Hello, this is Dial-a-joke. What can I do for you? Elephant joke? Sick joke? Gross joke? Little moron joke? Green pickle joke?"

"No, no, no, no," Emily said, but she was smiling.

April 18

Dear Mr. Diment,

Hi again! I wrote you a letter a while ago about your wonderful book, Paris Plus, which my girl friend and I have both read. I also asked you for the name of the guy on the cover of the book. No, I haven't changed my mind!

I still want it! I hope you'll send me the information soon.

I was just wondering if you got my first letter. I hope so! Sometimes the mail is not so reliable. For instance, my grandmother writes me about once a month, and last year two of her letters got lost. One had my birthday check in it, too. (Groan!)

I'd like to ask you a question. I was wondering how you write your books. I mean, is it inspiration? Do you suddenly get the idea and sit down and write it?

I've noticed something about trying to be funny (which made me wonder if that's like writing a book). Sometimes, I can be funny right off the top of my head. But sometimes (for instance, right now I'm working on a clown routine for a party), I have to figure out what I'm going to do, and then I have to do it in my room in front of the mirror and then I have to practice it to get it right.

This sort of worries me. Is it still funny if I practice it? That's why I asked you about inspiration.

Well, thanks for reading my letter. I'm sorry to take up your time, because I know someone like you must be pretty busy.

Your friend,

B. Larrabee

P.S. I don't mean to be a pest, so please excuse me, if you did get my first letter. If you did, you can just throw this one in the wastebasket. You won't hurt my feelings.

Chapter 6

Friday, the weather suddenly got hot. It was like a summer day. Mr. Cooper took our gym class outside. "Okay, let's get a little spirit into this group."

Emily and I agree that around Mr. Cooper, we always feel like slobs. One thing is the way he dresses. His shorts and T-shirts are always knock-your-eye-out white. He could do an ad on tv. "I use Drift for all my sweaty shorts and musty T-shirts." Another thing is his muscles. They're everywhere.

First he had us doing sit-ups and push-ups, then sprints around the track. Emily and I ran together. "You sure you don't want to go to the concert with me tonight?" I said.

"Lulu Belle Smith? No way."

"You might like it. Don't be so prejudiced."

She shook her head. She was huffing and puffing more than usual.

"You sound like an old rusty engine." I gave her a little bump.

"Don't."

I took a good look at her. Her face was kind of white and sweaty. "Are you feeling sick?"

"I'm okay."

Emily never likes to make a fuss. I kept looking at her. Gradually she went from white and sweaty to green and sweaty. "Emily, you look like an abused chicken."

She didn't even try to smile.

I got off the track and ran over to Mr. Cooper. "Emily's sick, Mr. C. She ought to go to the nurse. I can take her."

He stood there thinking about it, combing his fingers through his blond hair. "What's her problem?"

"I don't know. She looks like she's going to throw up." Just as I said it, Emily stumbled off the track and sat down with her head drooping.

Mr. Cooper went over to her. "Bunny's going to take you to the nurse."

When we got into the dispensary, Mrs. Voynis took one look at Em and stuck a thermometer in her mouth. "Hundred and one," she said, when she pulled it out. "Just enough to earn you a day or two in bed."

"I can't be sick tomorrow," Emily said. "That's my sister's and brother's birthday."

"Sorry, dear, bad timing. Can your mother come get you now?"

"No. She's working until six o'clock tonight."

"Well, come on, lie down for a while."

I went to the office and called my mom at work. The dispatcher got her on the beeper. Mom said she'd be at school in about an hour and drive Emily home. So that was okay.

I went back to the dispensary and sat down on the edge of the cot and talked to Emily. Nothing much. Just stuff to keep her from thinking about how crummy she felt.

"You have to go back to your class, Bunny," Mrs. Voynis said.

"It's just gym." I stayed until Emily fell asleep.

That night, after supper, I called Emily. Mrs. Boots said she was sleeping. "When she wakes up, I'll tell her you. . . . And oh! Your mother, Bunny. Thank you. Thank her." Mrs. Boots always talks in sort of half sentences. Since I've known her practically my whole life, I can usually understand what she's getting at.

"How does Emily feel, Mrs. Boots?"

"Not so. . . . But that's okay. It's going around, and by tomorrow. . . ."

When I hung up, I went upstairs and showered and got dressed for the concert. "I borrowed your bird earrings," I said to Mom when I came downstairs. She was waiting for me in the hall. She was driving me downtown. "Is that okay?" I had my hair in two braids. I was wearing a new purple blouse, a grape-colored vest, and a bunch of necklaces.

Dad came out of his study with his coffee cup in his hand. He stopped and looked at me. "Where're you going?"

"I told you at supper. To the concert."

He kissed the top of my head. "You look very nice. Is Mom picking you up afterward?"

"No, Dad, I'm going to hitch a ride home."

"You're *what?*"

"Bill, you're such an easy target," Mom said. "Shad, where are you?" she yelled. "You want to drive downtown with us?"

We went out to the garage. "How come Emily's not going with you?" Shad said, as we got in the car.

"She hates this kind of music. Anyway, she got sick in school today."

"Anything catching?" Shad asked. He sounded hopeful.

"Not for me. I'm so healthy, I never get anything."

At the Civic Center, Mom said, "Okay, I'll see you right out here at ten-thirty, Bunny. Right?"

"Right." I started to get out of the car.

"Bunny." Mom held up her face. I kissed her on the cheek. Shad stuck out his hand. I shook his hand. Then Mom took my face between her hands and smacked me on the lips. "Have fun."

I got out of the car and walked away fast, before Mom could yell after me to blow my nose and not talk to strangers. People were milling around all over the plaza outside, and inside it was even more jammed. Everybody seemed to be with somebody else. I wished Emily was with me.

The theater was so packed, I almost didn't get a seat. I saw an empty place and started to slide in toward it. A woman shook her head. "I'm saving this seat." The next empty seat I found, it was the same thing. "Taken. She's coming right back."

Finally I found a seat about halfway down, over on the left side. It was the last one in the row, right behind a post.

When Lulu Belle's band came out on the stage, everybody started clapping and yelling and whistling, even though Lulu Belle wasn't even in sight yet. I put two fingers in my mouth and whistled. The piano player (male), two electric guitar players (male and female), and a drummer (female) started tuning their instruments. They were all wearing loose white pants, jewelry around their necks, and sparkling purple shirts. Purple and white are Lulu Belle's colors.

The person next to me said something. I turned to answer him and then I just stared. He looked like the guy on the cover of *Paris Plus*. I don't mean he looked exactly like him, but enough so you could think he was at least Paris's brother. The same wavy, dark hair, the same long eyelashes, the same drop-dead eyes.

He was leaning way back in his seat, with his arms crossed over his chest. Everything about him was like Paris, including the way he was dressed, as if it was summer and hot, instead of early spring and cool. He was wearing khaki shorts, a shirt open at the neck, and a pair of beat-up sneakers.

"Have you been to a Lulu Belle concert before?" he asked.

I shook my head. He was so good-looking I just wanted to stare.

"My first time, too." He rolled his eyes. "Don't you wonder what we're in for?"

"Really," I said, because I couldn't think of anything else to say.

He was looking at me the way I wanted to look at him. I mean, he just *looked* at me, without turning away, sort of smiling and looking, as if he was interested in me. My whole face got hot. I could tell he was much older than I was. Would he be interested in *me*?

Suddenly I thought, Did I clean my ears when I took my shower? I got really anxious, and at the same time, I had this terrific impulse to laugh. It was a feeling like a sneeze coming. I tried to think of something to say, something good. Maybe something funny.

"How long have you been a Lulu Belle fan?" he said.

"About five years. How about you?"

"Oh, I'm just here on a fluke. I'm filling in for a friend who writes a column for our school paper."

"A music column?" A stupid joke popped into my mind. *You know what the weather report is from South America? Chile today.*

"No, just general stuff on the teen scene. My friend couldn't come tonight, so she asked me to sub for her. Which means I have to write the column." He looked around the theater. "I'm supposed to interview typical fans. Teens, like us."

Like *us*? I wondered how old he thought I was. Another stupid joke came into my head. *What did one cigarette say to the other? Take me to your lighter.* I almost said it. He was looking at me again. I almost said, Want to hear a joke? But just then, lucky for me, the lights dimmed, and Lulu Belle came out on the stage.

She looked beautiful. Her hair was down all around her shoulders, swinging loose. She was all in white, except for a crown of purple flowers on her head.

The first song she sang was my favorite of all her songs, "Don't Wait Up for Me Another Night." All the time she was singing, I couldn't think of anything else. Well, that's not totally true. Every once in a while, I'd turn just a little and focus on the guy next to me (in my mind I called him Paris's brother); I'd catch him out of the corner of my eye, and every time I'd be surprised at how good-looking he was. A couple of times, just when I did it, he was looking at me, too.

At the intermission, the whole audience got up and started moving around. People were talking to each other, and way in back, some people were singing a Lulu Belle song. A girl in a gray skirt was dancing by herself in the aisle.

I felt like dancing, too. If Emily had been with me, I think I would have, but instead I just stood up and sort of stretched and rolled my shoulders.

Paris's "brother" looked around and stretched, too. He was shorter than me. He sat down on the back of his upraised seat. He had strong-looking, hairy legs. I fiddled with the strings on my pocketbook. I wondered how old he was. He kept looking at me. He *was* looking at my ears.

I put my hand up casually to my ear and covered it. "How many people do you have to talk to?"

"I don't know." He looked uncertain. "I have

this awful feeling that I'm not going to be very good at this. I don't know why I said I'd do it. Curiosity maybe.''

"Or maybe you're so cheap, you couldn't resist a free ticket." I couldn't believe I'd said that. Typical Bunny, anything-for-a-joke bit.

But he laughed. "Could be. I'm not the world's biggest spender. . . . Where do you go to school?"

"Drumlins."

"I have some friends in Drum."

The cool way he said that — *Drum* — I knew he meant the high school, not the middle school. So he did think I was older!

"Do you know Laura Olsher?"

"No."

"Keith Reitson?" He was looking at my ears again! "He's a neat guy. . . . Well, I guess I ought to get up and talk to some people." But he didn't move. "I like your earrings," he said suddenly. "They're different."

I was so relieved that he was looking at my earrings and not into my ear, that I gave him a really big smile. "They're pretty, aren't they? Zuni Indian good luck charms." I didn't say I'd borrowed them from my mother. That sounded so young.

He smiled back. "Do you like Indian stuff?"

"I don't know that much about it. We got these in a gift shop in Nyack, New York."

He laughed. "Do you always tell the truth? You just blew your big chance to impress me. . . . I didn't tell you my name, did I? I'm James."

I don't know what happened to me next. I was

more relaxed. I didn't actually think what I was going to say. I just said it. "I'm Emily." I got a shock the moment I said it.

"Hi, Emily," James said.

Another shock, hearing him say it. Why had I done that? Maybe something had flashed through my mind — a thought, or half a thought. *Don't tell him your stupid name.* So I said Emily's name. But, really, it was something I did without thought. My impulsive self.

"So, what kind of school is Drum, Emily? I go to Sherwood. It's a decent school."

I said something or other. *I'm Emily.* I kept hearing myself say that.

"You know what, Emily?" James said. "Why don't I start by interviewing you for my article?" He sat down and so did I. "Let's see. . . ." He leaned on the arm of the seat, facing me. "Umm . . . tell me, Emily, what did you think of the show so far?"

"I liked it."

"Okay. Can you say anything else?" He pushed his hair out of his face. "Do you mind doing this?"

"No. I always wanted to be interviewed."

"Terrific." James cleared his throat. "Emily, give me your frank, woman-in-the-street opinion. Is hearing Lulu Belle in concert as good as listening to her records?"

"It's better! Much, much better." I kept thinking, Tell him your name isn't Emily. But I didn't. What did it matter? It wasn't like it was a big lie or something that would hurt anyone.

"You say it's better to listen to Lulu Belle in

person. Could you enlarge on that for our readers, please?"

"First, I get to see the band. Then there's Lulu Belle, herself. I don't think her record covers do her justice. She's beautiful. Don't you love her hair?"

"Yeah, it's pretty nice hair," he said.

"It's *great* hair."

"I can see you're a real fan. Can you tell me what you like so much about Lulu Belle?"

"Well, she has a voice that's husky and beautiful. Her songs are very well written. They're sad and beautiful." I thought that sounded pretty good. "Aren't you going to write any of this down?"

"James, boy reporter, forgot to bring a pad and pencil, but don't worry, Emily, I have a great memory."

All through the second half of the concert, I kept sneaking glances at James. I really liked him.

When the concert was over, Lulu Belle threw kisses to the audience. "I love ya all. I love ya all."

The lights came on. James was laughing. He put his head down in his hands. "Emily, admit it, Lulu Belle is corny."

"No, I'll never say it."

"I like a woman who sticks to her convictions, Emily."

Every time he said *Emily*, I got goosebumps. It was partly because of what I'd done, using Emily's name, but more because of the way James said it. He'd look right at me, smile just a little, and say it. *Emily*.

We walked up the aisle together. I wondered if

I'd ever see him again. Probably not. I tried to think of something sophisticated to say. *It's been a pleasure. . . . I guess this is good-bye. . . . Call me sometime. . . .* Suddenly, I said, "Did you ever think of calling yourself Paris?"

"What?"

"Nothing." I talked fast to cover my confusion. "Did you get enough for your article just interviewing me? Probably not. Why don't you just write what you really feel about Lulu Belle? I mean, if you didn't like the concert, you could just say so."

"That's a good idea. Maybe I'll do that."

We got caught in a traffic jam near the doors leading out to the lobby. James bent his head toward me. "Good thing crowds don't bother us."

We were standing really close. My ears were hot, and my neck, and then the back of my knees started burning. All of a sudden, I thought, Maybe I'm falling in love.

The traffic jam broke, and we moved toward the big glass entrance doors. One part of me wanted to stay back with him. The other part of me was thinking that my mother would be outside, waiting for me. I didn't want her to see me coming out with James, and I definitely didn't want James to see me getting in the car with her, like a watched-over infant. Besides, what if he yelled, " 'Bye, Emily"?

I started walking faster. Then I thought, When am I ever going to see him again? I slowed down. "James, can I see the article when you're done?"

"If I ever get it done. Maybe I should have asked you more questions."

"You could call me up."

"What's your phone number?"

I gave him my number. I said it automatically. Then I thought, Oh, no, he can't call my house and ask for Emily. Everything began to seem complicated. "I've got to go now," I said, and I pushed through the crowd, weaving in and out, as if I were playing basketball and dribbling down the court.

"Hey, Emily."

I heard him behind me. I turned around and waved, then I kept going.

Outside, Mom's car was right there, waiting at the curb. I got in. "Hi, sweetie. Was the concert good?"

"Yeah, I liked it." Clumps of people were all over the sidewalk. People kept coming out of the Civic Center. I saw James come out. I slumped down in the seat. "Let's go, Mom."

Mom turned on the key. The engine sputtered and didn't catch.

James was looking up and down the street. Was he looking for me? The back of my knees got hot again.

Mom slapped the dashboard. "Come on, baby." The engine caught and she pulled out into traffic.

I turned around and took one last look at James.

Chapter 7

The next morning, the first thing I thought of when I woke up was James. In my mind, I went over everything that had happened. I lay in bed and whispered to myself — what he said, what I said. My dad walked by my room. "Did you say something, Bunny?"

"No, Dad." I pulled the covers over my head. I remembered how James had said my name — I mean, Emily's name. But he thought it was mine. He was saying it that way for me. Looking right at me, then a little smile. *Emily*. It was still weird to remember that I'd used Emily's name. Could you be in love with somebody who didn't know your real name? What if he'd asked me my last name? Would I have said Boots? Or Larrabee? Emily Larrabee. It sounded nice.

After a while I got out of bed. Today was the twins' birthday party. I wanted to practice my clown routine some more. I put on an old shirt of my father's over my pj's and practiced falling down and running up a wall. Doing a good fall was really hard.

I stood in front of the mirror and tried to make up my mind which kind of clown I would be, sad or happy. I still hadn't decided. I looked in the mirror, made a sad face. Bottom lip stuck out, eyes squinty, forehead wrinkled.

My mother looked in. "Bunny, what are you doing? Aren't you coming down for breakfast?"

"Soon." I tried the happy face — big turned-up lips, lots of teeth, wide open eyes. I decided on the happy face, because that seemed more natural for me.

I went downstairs and ate breakfast. My mind was going like this: James. . . . Too bad I can't juggle four tennis balls. . . . James. . . . Should practice falling down more. . . . James. . . . Can't tell any jokes, 'cause clowns are silent. . . . James. . . .

When I was ready to go, I asked Mom if I should put on my clown costume here or if I should get dressed at Emily's house.

"Put it on here," she said. "That would be fine."

"Everybody would see me. I'd look like a freak."

"A clown isn't a freak. Everyone loves a clown, sweetie."

"I'll get dressed at Emily's."

Emily used to live three blocks away. But after the divorce, Mrs. Boots had to sell their house and move. Now they live in an apartment building, about a mile away.

When I got to Emily's house, the landlord, Mr.

Linaberry, was out in the yard. He's a little bald man. He always looks at me suspiciously, like I'm going to rob his house. And no matter how many times I tell him my name, he always says, "Hello, you."

"Hello, Mr. Linaberry. I'm Bunny, Emily's friend."

"Hello, you."

I ran upstairs. Mrs. Boots opened the door for me. "Hello, Mrs. Boots. Am I late?" I peered around. I didn't see any little kids. No Wilma and Chris. And Mrs. Boots was wearing an old bathrobe. "Mrs. Boots? The party — ?"

"We called off. . . . Didn't I — "

"You didn't tell me, Mrs. Boots."

"You're sure?" she said. "Last night, I was calling everyone and — I talked to you, didn't I?"

"Yes, Mrs. Boots, but I called you, to ask how Emily was."

"Oh, Bunny, I'm sorry." She gave me a kiss. "Oh, Bunny, you came for. . . . And I didn't even! I'm terrible."

"That's okay, Mrs. Boots. I don't care."

"Who is it, Ma?" Emily called from her bedroom.

"It's me, Em."

"Bunny. Come on in." I went in. Emily was sitting up in bed. She had a box of tissues next to her and a grocery bag for a wastebasket taped to the edge of her bed. There was a pitcher of juice on the bed table.

"I didn't know you were still sick," I said.

"Not just me," she croaked. She blew her nose. "We all got sick. Wilma and Chris, too. No pardy. They were throwing up all night."

I cleared stuff off her bureau and hoisted myself

up. "So guess what?" I said. "I went to the concert last night."

"I had a big evening, too. I slept and when I wadn't sleeping, I wadched teevee." She sneezed. "How was it?"

"Great." I wanted to tell her about James, but I didn't know where to start. "Where's my book *Paris Plus*?" I said. I could show her the cover. *Guess what, Emily? I met a guy last night who looks like Paris's brother. I told him my name was Emily. And something else, Emily. I think I might be in love with him.*

Emily waved vaguely. "Your book's somewhere in this mess. I didn't finish it yet. You still like old, corny Lulu Belle? 'I love ya allll,' " she croaked.

"Em-ily."

"Well, Buddy, she is *so* corny."

"I know, Emily, you always say that."

"Because it's the trudth."

"That's what this guy said, too." I waited. Emily didn't catch on. She didn't say, What guy? Her ears didn't perk up. She really was sick!

"Corny." She sneezed three times. "Corny. Corny." She blew her nose.

"Emily, if you weren't such a sick chicken, I'd kill you."

"Do it!" Bloodthirsty little Wilma came in. Right behind her was Chris. They were both in pj's.

"Hello, Wilma. . . . Hey, ugly face." I ruffled up Chris's hair.

"Don't." He smoothed out his hair.

"What do you two guys want, anyway?" I said. "Go away, I'm talking to Emily."

"You can talk. We won't stop you," Chris said.

"Maybe I don't want you to hear what I'm saying. Don't you have anything to do? Why don't you go throw up?"

"Yeech," Wilma said. She sat down on Emily's bed. "What's in your knapsack, Bunny?" She opened my sack and started pawing through it.

"Go right ahead, Wilma. Don't ask permission or anything. That's fine with me." My sarcasm was lost on her. Wilma thinks I half belong to her, anyway.

"What's all this stuff, Bunny? What is it? Is this your clown stuff?"

"Clown stuff! Neat!" Chris said. "Can I see it?"

I took out the pants, which were an old pair of my father's, from when he was really fat. I was only going to show them to Wilma and Chris, but then I pulled them on over my jeans and hopped around, holding them up. The twins, and Emily, too, thought that was pretty funny.

That got me going. I put on the flowered shirt and the old felt hat I'd found in our attic, wrapped a tie around my neck, and shoved my feet into a pair of Mom's shoes. Her feet are even bigger than mine.

Chris stood up on the bed and shouted, "Bunny! You are so funny!"

That was all the encouragement I needed. I went into the bathroom and put on my makeup. White face. Big red, smiling lips. Dark lines around my eyes. I tied string around the pants to hold them up, and, finally, I put on a pair of extra-large-size rubber gloves that I'd stuffed with tissue paper.

I went down the hall and back into Emily's room. The shoes flapped with every step.

Emily sneezed and said, "Buddy, thad's a wod-derful costume."

"Where'd you get those hands?" Chris said.

I didn't say a word. Just went into my clown act. First thing I did was fall over my own feet. I stumbled around, got my legs tangled up, fell again, rolled over, got up, flapped around the room, waving my arms. Chris and Wilma were laughing so hard I kept it going longer than I'd planned. It was great. It was so much fun.

I kept falling, trying to get to my feet, sprawling my legs out and flopping around like a fish on the floor. Mrs. Boots came and stood in the doorway. My finale was juggling three oranges in my big yellow hands.

"Well, Bunny," Mrs. Boots said, "that's just. . . . It really is!"

They all clapped for me. I took another bow, fell over my feet again, looked sad, and crawled out of the room. Then I popped my head around the side of the door and flapped my rubber hands in a good-bye wave. That part I just made up on the spot. I guess you would call it inspiration.

Chapter 8

On the way home I was thinking that maybe I'd go to clown college when I graduated high school. There's a clown college in Florida. There're a lot of things to learn if you want to be a real clown. It can be a lifetime profession. All at once I realized two important things had happened to me. I fell in love, and I was figuring out what I was going to do with my life.

"Hello, I'm home," I yelled, when I walked into the house. I dumped my knapsack in the living room and I went into the kitchen. Shad was fixing a sandwich and feeding one of his gerbils.

"Where's Mom?" I said.

"Shopping." He petted the gerbil. "It's okay, it's okay, honey. What were you yelling about, Bunny? You made Benjie nervous."

"So sorry, Benjie. Where's Dad?"

"Working in his study. You can't go in there. He said not to bother him for anything. He's trying to finish an article."

The phone rang. "Answer it," I said. I poured myself a glass of milk.

Shad picked up the phone. "Hello? No, there's no Emily here. You've got the wrong number." He hung up.

I almost choked on the milk.

"Second time asking for Emily," Shad remarked. "Must be the same guy as before." He took a jar of Vitamin C out of the cupboard and poured out a handful. "I think Benjie could use some vitamin therapy. Did you know calcium has a calming effect?" He took some calcium pills, then threw in a few wheat germ capsules. "I'm going to give him one of each of these twice a day."

"Very good, doctor. You got the same wrong number twice?"

"Uh huh."

"Why'd he ask for Emily?"

"How do I know? It's a wrong number."

It was James calling. I just knew it was him calling. "Was it a guy or a girl on the phone?"

"Guy." Shad put the pill bottles back into the cupboard.

"And he had the wrong number?"

Shad looked at me like I was mentally defective. "Do you know any Emilys that live here?"

I sat down at the kitchen table. *Sure, I do, Shad. Me!* "Did he say his name?"

"I told you, it was a wrong number."

"I know, I just meant, sometimes people say, Well, this is so and so."

The phone rang again. Shad looked disgusted. "That bozo. He's calling again."

"I'll get it, Shad. You go take care of Benjie." I started to pick up the phone, then waited until Shad left the room. "Hello?"

"Hello, is Emily there?"

It was him! My cheeks started burning. Then I panicked. I didn't know what to say. *Sure, this is Emily. No, this is Bunny, but I'm the one you want.* "This is — " I sort of muffled my voice. "Who did you want?"

"Emily. I, um, I don't know her last name, but I know I've got the right number."

"Oh, Emily. Ahh, yes. Just a moment." I needed time to think.

Shad came back into the kitchen. "Who is it?" he said.

I covered the phone with my hand. "No one. None of your business." I shouldn't have said it. Not to bulldog Shad.

"Boy or girl?"

"Shad. Does it matter?"

"Is it Emily? Can I talk to her?"

I looked down at the phone and clamped my hand over the mouthpiece tighter. "It's somebody from school."

He knew I was lying. He got this silly smile on his face. "Who is it? Let me say hello."

"No! Shad, will you please go? This is personal."

"It's not Emily? I'll go if you tell me who it is."

"Shad!"

"It must be a boy, if it's so personal."

"Shad Larrabee, if you don't leave this minute — " I tried the same thing on him that I'd done with Wilma. " — I'm going to haunt you."

Didn't bother him in the least. "You could do it," he said, "you've got the face for it."

"Shad! I mean it! Go!" He left at last. I closed the kitchen door, took a big breath, and unclamped my hand from the phone. "Hello?"

"Emily?"

"Yes."

"Hi! It's me, James. From last night."

"You remembered my number."

"I told you, I have a good memory. Who was I talking to before, your sister?"

"Uh, yes, and before that my little brother."

"Little joker, isn't he? I called you twice and twice he said you didn't live there."

"He did? He does things like that sometimes."

"Well, I just called to say hello, and I thought I'd ask you a few more questions about Lulu Belle. Hey, it was fun last night. Never thought I'd enjoy a Lulu Belle concert."

"Oh. Well, do you like her any better now?"

"I'll tell you. She's pure corn, but good corn."

"Creamed corn," I said.

"Listen, Emily? I hope you don't think I always go around picking up girls."

"Oh, no."

He laughed. "But I do. But only cute ones, like you."

All of a sudden, I thought, What if Dad picks up the phone in the study and hears this? He'll want to know everything! "James? I can't talk right now. In fact, I'm sorry, but I shouldn't have given you my phone number. I mean, you really can't call me here."

"Why not?"

"Well . . . you just can't — My parents . . . they're, uh, they're peculiar about the phone. They're, uh, they have rules about the phone."

He groaned. "You, too, Emily? Tell me about it! My old man is a total nutcase when he gets on the subject of the telephone. Are they on you about the phone bill?"

"No, it's not that so much. Just — my father needs it for his work, and — " I was stumbling, making it up as I went along. "I have to call all my friends, actually, from pay phones."

"Mondo bizarro," he said. "They sound worse than my parents. Why don't you call me back? Pick a time when they're not around, or they're not using the phone, or whatever."

"Okay," I said. "Yes. I will."

He gave me his phone number. "It's an easy one."

"Yes." I kept checking the door and listening for that little click on the phone that tells you someone else is on.

"When's a good time for you?" he said. "I want to talk to you some more about that article. How about tomorrow afternoon?"

Sunday. If I went out to use a pay phone, Mom would say, Bunny, today's a day for us all to be home together.

"Not tomorrow."

"Busy?"

"Yes."

"Date?"

"Umm, not really."

"I know what you mean."

56

He did? I didn't. "How about Monday?"

"No, I work Monday, Emily. Tuesday, around four o'clock?"

"Okay."

"Great talking to you again, Emily. Hey, I really liked those earrings."

"Zuni bird charms," I said.

"I know. I remember. Bye-bye, Emily-braids."

" 'Bye," I said weakly.

Chapter 9

I meant to tell Emily about James. I was going to do it first thing Monday, when I saw her. We met by the window on the second floor. "Hello, sickey," I said. "You feeling okay now?"

"Pretty good."

She didn't look that good to me. She looked like what my mother calls green around the gills. It probably didn't help that she was wearing a green sweater.

"Your clown act must have cured the twins, Bunny. After you left, Mom said they got better so fast she couldn't believe it. She promised them another party over vacation."

"I'll be in Toronto with my grandmother."

"I know. I have to figure out something else good."

"Let the little monsters play some games. Pin the Tail on the Donkey, or — "

The bell rang and we had to run for it. That was the way it went all day. Every time I started to tell Emily about James, either we talked about something else, or something happened to stop me or — I finally realized — I stopped myself.

Why? Two things. First, I was sort of worried how Emily would feel about my using her name. I didn't know if she'd be mad, or what. I started arguing with her in my head. *Look, Em, if you used my name, I wouldn't be mad.* But that was ridiculous. Why would anybody want to use my name?

Then, I was uneasy about telling her how much I liked James. I guess I thought it was sort of traitorous of me. Here we went around all the time saying, *Nobody* falls in love at our age! I mean, it was something *we* didn't care about. Not yet. And now I'd done it.

I walked home with Emily after school. I didn't say anything about James. Instead, I started going on about my sister, Star. She'd called home the night before and talked to Mom again. A whole hour on the phone and not one word to me!

"It really burns me, Emily. Mom says Star has things on her mind. But does that mean she has to act like I don't exist?"

"I wonder if I'll be like that with Chris and Wilma."

"No, you won't. You're too nice. You're not self-centered like my sister."

When we got to Emily's house, she sat down at the kitchen table. "Whew. I feel so dragged." She put her head down on her arms. "You want something to eat, Bunny?"

"Yes." I took a box of graham crackers out of the cupboard.

Emily picked up her head. "You know what I wish I could do? Get in bed and sleep for about fifteen hours."

"Why don't you?"

She shook her head. "The twins'll be home in a couple of minutes. I have to make supper for them. Mom doesn't get home till six today. They go berserk if they don't eat before that."

I opened the refrigerator and took out the butter. "I'll make supper for them."

"You?"

"Hey, Emily. You're not the only one who can do things, you know."

"I don't mean that. Why should you cook for my sister and brother? It's my job." Her voice was wavery.

I took a good look at her. She had that green, fishy color around the eyes again. "Dummy! Will you shut up and go take a rest?"

"Don't call me dummy. And don't keep telling me to shut up." All of a sudden, she started to cry.

Then I knew she was still sick. I pulled a chair over and sat down next to her. "Em." I put my arm around her shoulders. "Go get in bed," I said, in my best Nurse Nancy voice. "And wipe your nose." I handed her a napkin. "This is like kindergarten, isn't it?"

"I know." She giggled, blew her nose, and started crying again. I finally got her to go to her room and lie down. About two minutes later, the twins blew in. They each had a little knapsack on their backs.

"Hi, guys." I told them I was going to cook their supper.

"You?" Wilma said.

"You?" Chris echoed.

"It better be good," Wilma said.

"Hey, it'll be the best supper you ever ate, Wilma."

"Are you going to juggle oranges?" Chris asked.

"Maybe. We'll see." I was trying to remember what kids their age liked to do. I thought I'd have to amuse them, play games with them, do my clown act, keep them from wrecking the house, but after I gave them graham crackers and milk, they sat down at the kitchen table like two little pussycats and did homework.

I got my own homework out. I kept peeking over the top of my notebook to see if they were going to suddenly explode. I kept my eye on Wilma, especially, but she was the one who told Chris he had to finish. "Or no tv tonight. You know what Mom said."

Emily had told me to make them — ugh — salmon patties. When I started fixing the food, I told Chris to set the table and Wilma to sweep the floor.

"We don't have to take orders from you, Bunny."

"Yeah, you do, if you want to eat supper."

When Mrs. Boots came home, Emily was still sleeping and the kids were eating dessert. I'd made them Jell-O.

"Bunny, did you eat?" Mrs. Boots said.

"No, thanks, Mrs. Boots."

"No, no, the least I can. . . . Bunny, please . . . there's plenty here." She pulled off her shoes and massaged her feet.

"No, really, Mrs. Boots — "

"But I insist. After all you've. . . . Sit down, Bunny. Mmm, these salmon patties you made look delicious. Here's bread. Do you want a glass of milk?" She started serving me. I didn't know how to tell her I hated salmon patties, so I ate two of them.

The next day, Emily felt better. Lunchtime, I decided I'd definitely tell her about James. But I just didn't get to it.

Mr. Pelter and Ms. Linsley came into the cafeteria together, and we started gossiping about our teachers. "She doesn't even look like a teacher," Emily said. "They're cute together, aren't they?"

Later, in study hall, I wrote Emily a note.

Dear Emily,

I want to talk to you. Have something to tell you. Make sure I tell you. Meet you after school, the usual place.

Love, Bunny

We met on the steps near the parking lot. "Well," I said, "don't kill me for not telling you right away, but I met a guy at the concert. And today I have to call him."

We started walking. "You met a guy?" Emily said. "You mean, somebody you didn't know before?"

"His name is James. I met him at the concert."

"You said that already."

"I'll say it again. I met him at the concert."

"You picked him up?"

"No! Yes. I don't know, Em. I just talked to him."

"Was he cute?"

"Adorable!" I told her what he looked like, how he was dressed. I told her about the article and about his calling me at home. I told her every-thing — almost. I still left out the part about using her name! It was cowardly of me. I don't know what I was so afraid of. Maybe I wasn't afraid of anything. Maybe I just didn't want to hear Emily say something sensible like, Well, Bunny, just tell him your right name.

Also, though I said I really, really liked him, I didn't put in that I might be in love.

"At first you thought he was Paris?" She had a little smile on her face that I couldn't figure out.

"Almost. Wait until you meet him," I said, for-getting that she couldn't meet him, unless I was prepared to: 1. tell Emily I'd called myself Emily, and 2. tell James my name was actually Bunny, or, 3. tell Emily I'd used her name, and 4. let James go on thinking it was my name. I began to imagine the meeting.

James, I want you to meet my best friend. Her name is Emily.

Hello, Emily! Well, Emily, I'm glad Emily introduced me. So, Emily. Emily is your best friend? Emily, how long have you known Emily?

"How old did you say he was, Bunny?"

"I didn't," I said. "I guess, seventeen."

"Seventeen!"

"Maybe eighteen. He thought I was in high school, Em."

"When you get dressed up, you look older. It's probably being tall." She made a face. "Nobody ever thinks I'm older. What are you going to say when you call him?"

"I don't know. He said he wanted to talk about the article."

"Where are we going to call him from?"

"We?" I coughed. "Em, I hope you don't mind, but — " I didn't want to hurt her feelings. I slung my arm across her shoulder. "It would be better if I just called. I mean — it's embarrassing to have someone else listen."

"It's just me," Emily said.

"I know. But you know what I mean."

Emily shrugged.

"I'll call you tonight. Tell you what he said."

"You don't have to."

I stared at her. She had that odd little smile on her face. Was she jealous? "I want to call you tonight, Emily. I want to tell you about it. I'm not trying to keep this to myself. Why do you think I just told you everything?" All the time I was saying it, I felt like such a big liar. Because I hadn't told her everything at all. "Maybe I won't even get him," I added.

I phoned James from a pay phone outside a drugstore. He answered right away. "Well, here I am," I said. "Calling from a pay phone."

"Your timing is perfect, Emily. I'm working on that article right now. I even went to the library and looked up Lulu Belle, so I know her whole story, how she was a poor girl from the hills of North Carolina, how she got her first job singing when she was ten years old on a local radio station, etcetera etcetera."

"I think she was eight years old," I said.

"And I talked it over with Maureen — "

"Who?" My face flushed.

"Maureen. My friend. Remember I said I was doing this for a friend? She tells me the background stuff is okay, but I need more personal stuff."

I leaned against the wall of the phone booth. "Well, if you give your opinion — "

"Yeah. Right. That's personal, but she meant more on the line of the kind of stuff we were talking about. When I was interviewing you. Maybe you could just tell me why you like Lulu Belle so much — "

"You know. I told you. I like her music."

"Right. Anything else? I'm just looking here for some little anecdote to spice up this column."

"Why don't you tell Maureen to write the column?" I blurted. "I mean, since you're having so much trouble."

He didn't say anything for a moment.

I thought I'd made him mad. Just like me, opening my big mouth. What if he hung up on me? Would I call him back? "James?" I said, very softly. He didn't answer. Then I started wondering if Maureen was his girl friend. Did he have more than one girl friend? He was so good-looking. He probably had two or three. I looked outside. It had just started to rain. A man was waiting for the phone, tossing a coin from one hand to the other.

"James?" I said again.

"Uh . . . sorry. I was just thinking about what you said. I guess this is a matter of pride. Didn't you ever say you'd do something, Emily, and then be sorry? But you went ahead and did it anyway? Just because of pride?"

I couldn't remember anything like that, exactly. Still, I knew what it was to want to do something really well. "I have this clown act I do," I said.

"A clown act?"

"Yes. I do things like pratfalls and juggling tennis balls. I like to tell jokes, but in this act — "

Just then, the operator broke in, or the computer — anyway, a voice saying I had to put in another quarter for two more minutes.

"Let me call you back," James said. I told him the number and hung up. The phone rang and I picked it up. The man with the coin gave me a mean look and walked away.

"Hi, there," James said.

"Hi." The raindrops on the top of the phone booth made a cozy sound.

"So, look, Emily, let's get back to Lulu Belle. Can't you think of some cute little story about you and Lulu Belle?"

"Well, let me think."

"Sure. Go ahead. Take your time. It's my dime."

I stood there, but I didn't think of anything. I wanted to help him, but my mind was blank. All of a sudden, I had a terrible thought. The only reason he was interested in me was because he needed my help in writing his article. "I don't have a story about Lulu Belle," I said. "I don't know her." I really felt sort of disgusted and upset.

I guess it was in my voice, because James said, "Emily? Are you okay, Emily?"

Just at that moment, I was ready to say, *My name isn't Emily! Stop calling me Emily!*

"You know what, Emily?" he said. "Why don't we just sit down together someplace and talk?"

"About what? The article?"

"Well, sure. Or we could talk about school, or we could talk about anything. How does that sound to you? Why don't we meet in Stanchio's in the mall, the gelato place? Where are you now?"

"You want to meet now?"

"Like my dad always says, 'No time like the present.' Are you anywhere near the mall? We don't have to meet there."

"I'm about two blocks away."

"You see! It's perfect. I could meet you in about ten minutes."

"Okay."

"Great. See you soon, Emily. Bring your money. You gotta buy me a gelato."

I hung up and started walking toward the mall. It was still raining. I thought, What am I doing? Then I tried not to think at all. I was excited and worried at the same time. I told myself it was stupid to be worried. I wasn't doing anything wrong. This wasn't a date. I was just meeting a friend to have some gelato and talk about a singer. That made me feel better.

It was raining a little harder and it reminded me of the first time I ever heard Lulu Belle sing. It was five years ago. The Rosenfelds, friends of Mom and Dad's, loaned us their trailer and we drove up to Iron Lake over the Memorial Day weekend.

It rained the whole time. We hardly ever got out of that little trailer. We ate popcorn, played gin rummy, and listened to the radio.

I was lying in bed the last night, listening to the rain smacking on the metal roof of the trailer. Star was reading on the bunk below me. Shad was playing on the other bunk, and Mom and Dad were talking up front. Their voices were like bees.

I was lying there, drowsy, sleepy, wishing we never had to leave. And then I heard Lulu Belle singing "Mama, I Didn't Mean What I Said, Dear." And I just fell in love with her voice.

I was at Stanchio's first. I waited outside. I wanted to see James before he saw me. I kept wondering if my memory of him was right. Maybe he wasn't so good-looking. Maybe he wasn't so nice. Maybe I'd been totally wrong about his character.

I watched the people going up and down the aisle. Lots of couples. Mothers with their kids. Suddenly two boys came roller-skating down the aisle with a security guard running after them. "I guess roller-skating isn't allowed," someone said in my ear.

I turned around. It was James. I wasn't exactly paralyzed with shock, but it was a pretty close imitation. Here he was, looking as gorgeous as the first time I'd seen him. The back of my knees started that weird burning. And my face got hot. "Hi," I said. I don't know how I managed to sound so normal.

"Did you wait long?"

"No, that's okay."

We walked in and sat down at a little round table. "What are you going to get?" James said.

"I always order raspberry," I said.

"No, you've got to be more adventurous than that." We got up and went to the counter and tasted about twelve different flavors on the little wooden sticks before we made up our minds.

"Sit down, folks," the man behind the counter said. He had a bald, brown, freckled head. "I'll bring your gelatos to the table."

We sat down again and I told James about the camping weekend when I'd first heard Lulu Belle sing. I didn't think it was so special, but he really liked it.

"Emily, that's great. That's what I needed. Now I just have to write the thing."

We sat there and talked for about an hour. I really liked him. I liked him more than ever. At first I couldn't forget how handsome he was, but after a while, I did. I know that sounds funny, but what I mean is, I stopped concentrating on his gorgeous looks and liked him for his personality.

"Maureen says the next time she needs someone to fill in for her, it's not going to be me. She says I'm more trouble as a reporter than I'm worth."

"Is she your girl friend?"

"We're friends. Of course, I'm probably ruining our friendship by doing this article. I'm taking so long, Maureen says she could have written five articles by now."

"I guess you're not interested in journalism."

"Me? I guess not. This was supposed to be a lark. It was fun, too. I met you. Of course, I had to sit through an entire Lulu Belle Smith concert. Which, you gotta admit, is a big price to pay."

"I admit nothing."

He laughed. I really liked to see him laugh. Maybe I should tell him a joke. If I could think of a good one, I would. *What'd the mother ear of corn say when the baby ear of corn asked where he came from? The stalk brought you.* I put my hand over my mouth, so I wouldn't even be tempted to open it.

"No, I'm not going anywhere near journalism," James said. "I'll probably go to law school."

"Oh."

"Oh. Oh? Is that all you can say? Don't you think I'd make a good lawyer?"

"How do I know?"

He put his hand over mine. "Emily, there's something about you that I really like. I don't know what it is. You're different. . . ."

That worried me. "What do you mean?"

"I don't know. Different. I like it. You're fun."

When we got up to leave, I said, "Don't forget, this is my treat."

"What do you mean?" He already had his wallet out.

"You said I was buying your gelato."

"Emily, I was just joking. I'll treat you."

"No, that's okay." I went right up to the counter and paid.

"Well, thank you," James said.

"You can treat me next time," I said.

"It's a deal," James said.

Chapter 10

School closed a few days later for spring vacation. I took the bus to Toronto to visit my grandmother. It's a pretty long trip, about six hours, but I didn't mind too much. Mom gave me a sackful of food, and I had some books and a miniature checker game with me. The worst part was customs. We all had to get out of the bus while the customs officers asked us questions. They took forever, and there was nothing to do but stand around watching the lines of cars coming into and going out of Canada.

In Toronto, Grandma was waiting for me at the bus station. We started talking the moment we saw each other. We hugged and kissed and talked, all at the same time. "New blouse?" I said. She was wearing a bright red, open-necked blouse with puffy sleeves.

"Do you like it? I have so many things planned

for us. Let me look at you!" Grandma talks with just a little Canadian accent, which I think is really neat. "Give me another kiss."

Grandma's apartment is on the fifth floor of the Queens Arms on Avenue Road, which is a really busy street. It's got four lanes of traffic. Two things you notice right away when you walk into Grandma's apartment: Her favorite colors are blue (couches and rugs) and cream (walls and curtains), and she loves flowers. She always has some kind of fresh flowers. When I got there, it was daisies in a blue vase.

The first thing she did was measure me. This is one of our traditions. She puts me up against the door frame and makes a mark. Then we check it against the mark from my last visit. "Six months, and you've grown a whole inch!" She doesn't care that I'm already taller than she is. She looked as pleased as if I'd invented orange juice.

Grandma used to be a social worker and my grandfather was an engineer. I hardly remember him, but I know what he looked like, from his pictures. At home we keep our pictures in the album, but Grandma has her family pictures everywhere. Even the top of the tv is covered with pictures. Most of them are of Star, Shad, and me. We're her only grandchildren, and Mom is her only child.

"My only living child," Grandma corrected me. We were eating supper on the table in front of the big front windows. "I had a little boy before your mother. He would have been your uncle, but he died."

"How old was he?" I thought of Shad.

"Two months."

"Well, that's not too bad," I said. Grandma looked at me. "I only meant it would be worse if he was older."

Grandma lit a cigarette. "No, darling, if you love somebody, age doesn't make a difference. Either way. My baby's name was Wade. When he died, I thought I was a bad mother, that little Wade died because I did something terrible and careless."

"What?"

"I don't know, I was just afraid it was my fault. We didn't know about Sudden Infant Death Syndrome then." She turned her head and blew smoke over her shoulder.

I wanted to change the subject. It was making Grandma sad. "Grandma, I thought you were going to give up the weed."

"Now, Bunny, don't start on me. I've smoked too long to give it up."

"You always say that."

"I'll say it again." Her voice gets very dignified when she doesn't want to lose an argument. "But don't you start, it's a terrible habit."

"Grandma. You always say that, too. Don't you know you're supposed to set an example for me?"

"I am. A bad example."

Grandma and I talk a lot. We talk at the table, and we talk when we're out together, and we talk in bed. I always sleep in Grandma's room in the extra twin bed. She tells me family stories and stories about when she was my age. "I remember in high school, we had a contest for Miss Homemaker. We had to make *blanc mange*, the worst stuff ever created!"

I love to hear Grandma tell this story. I never remind her that I've heard it before. The first time I heard it, I didn't know what *blaah maj* was. (That's the way she says it.) Now I know it just means white pudding.

"We had to fold socks for the contest, pack a suitcase, iron a tablecloth. Isn't that terrible? The only thing I'm proud of is that I didn't win!"

I tell her about school, and me and Emily. And I tell her jokes. The worse they are, the better she likes it. ("Grandma, did I tell you about the surgeon who liked to tell jokes? He had his patients in stitches.") One thing about Grandma, she never acts bored.

Maybe that's why I told her about James. And maybe I just wanted to talk about him. Every time I thought of him, I got that hot, sweaty feeling. Was that love? I wished I could ask Grandma, but even her I didn't tell everything. I just couldn't tell her about being in love. I didn't want to talk about that. It was something to think about privately.

"James sounds like a nice person," she said. "But, you have to be careful, darling. You can't just go around trusting *anybody*."

"I know. I could tell he wasn't a creep, Grandma."

"Good. Always use your good common sense."

I never mind when Grandma gives me advice. Sometimes she even says things out of the blue. "Bunny, if you want something, you take a stand."

"Okay." I waited for her to say something else, but that was it.

Two more things I should mention about Grandma. One is that she is fierce about Canada and, especially, Toronto being the best place in the world to live. The other is that she's a baseball fanatic. Maybe I should say a Toronto Blue Jays fanatic.

The second night I was there, we went to a game at Exhibition Stadium. We walked up the long, winding concrete ramps. For some reason, I really like doing that. There was a huge crowd. Our seats were in Row 32, right behind first base. "I took care of us," Grandma said.

It was a pretty cold night, and Grandma had brought blankets for us to wrap around our legs. She had a pair of binoculars around her neck and snacks in a little red and white cooler.

The other team was introduced. The announcer called out their names in a flat voice. As they ran out on the field, some people applauded. Then the Jays were introduced. The announcer's voice boomed out over the stadium. "Ladies and gentlemen. Willeee. NELSON!" The crowd went crazy. They stood up, threw their fists in the air, and screamed. Grandma, too!

All through the game, Grandma yelled at our team. "Go, baby! Base hit, baby! You can do it." She groaned every time the Jays struck out or made an error. She jumped up and cheered and screamed every time the Jays did anything halfway good.

Afterward, even though it wasn't the best way to go home, we took the GO Train. "You always like doing this," Grandma said. She's right. The GO Train is a double-decker, and we rode on top.

"Isn't it excellent?" Grandma said. She sounded as if she were responsible. "It's clean, quiet, and smooth."

"Grandma, you're better than a commercial."

"I only speak the truth. There's nothing like this in the States, now is there?"

The conductor's voice came to us over the PA system. "Ladies and gentlemen. Sit back and relax. We have a little wait. I know it's late at night and you all want to get home. Talk to your neighbor or take a snooze. I'll wake you up when we get there."

Grandma poked me. "See? Do you have that in the States?"

The next day, Grandma was tired. First I thought I would hang around the apartment and wait for her to rest. I started to write a letter to Emily. But I didn't want to stay in, it seemed like a waste of my vacation. So I went out myself.

It's really easy to get around downtown Toronto. I could have taken the Metro, but I like walking, and Grandma lives only a few blocks from Yonge Street, which is like the main street. You could just go straight down Yonge Street, go in and out of stores and shops all you want, and never worry about directions.

Anyway, the people here are extremely nice. Even if I got lost, which I wouldn't, I wouldn't worry about it. I had a map with me. I like maps. I like knowing where I am. I walked around different parts of downtown. It seemed as if every time I took my map out, though, someone else stopped and asked me if I needed any help. The first person was a guy with a beard and a knapsack. He was tacking a notice for a sculpture show on a telephone pole. "That's my girl friend's show," he said. "She posts my notices — I'm a jazz musician — and I post hers."

The next time I took out my map, a woman wearing a fur coat stopped to ask me if I was okay, and the time after that it was a man who was selling hot dogs. "You need directions? Ask me. I know every street in Toronto."

I bought a hot dog from him. A woman was working with him. She smiled at me. "Nice girl." She was an old fat woman in a shabby dress, and she had no teeth. "Nice. Just like my granddaughter," she said, smiling at me with her toothless gums.

When I told Grandma about her later, she said, "Maybe that'll be me someday." She leaned on her hand. "I'll be really old, and toothless, and poor. Will you still come to visit me, then, Bunny?"

"Grandma! Your sense of humor is getting worse." I knew she was teasing, but I hated even hearing her talk about being old and poor.

"Sorry, darling." She hugged me. "Come, come, don't look like that. I'll get old so gradually, you'll hardly even notice. There, is that better?"

"No!"

"Okay, then tell me a joke," she said.

"Grandma, do you think I'm a joke machine?"

"Yes." She snapped her fingers. "And I'm your best audience."

"All right, let me think. . . . Okay." I grabbed the broom like a microphone. "The joke of the day, ladeez and genlemun, *is*, Why did the man go on a diet? Does anybody here want to try for the answer? That little lady there in the red silk blouse!" I pointed to Grandma. "Go ahead, little lady."

"Why?"

"Because, little lady, he didn't believe in the survival of the fattest."

"Oh, bad. Bad, bad, bad." Grandma groaned.

On my last day, Grandma said we should do so many things it would seem like two days to us. So we went out very early and had breakfast in a tiny French restaurant. I love that kind of breakfast and I can never have it at home. All we ate was fresh, hot French bread with butter, plus coffee for Grandma and hot chocolate with whipped cream for me.

"Do you make your own bread?" Grandma asked the woman behind the counter.

"*Oui.* Yes. *Du pain.*" She put the loaf on a wooden board. "Thick slices or small?"

"Small," Grandma said.

"Thick," I said.

"Listen to her," Grandma said.

"No, listen to her," I said.

The woman waited with her bread knife in the air.

"Grandma, you always give me my way. You shouldn't."

"And why not? It's my pleasure."

The woman smiled and cut the bread. We got thick slices.

After breakfast, we went to Kensington Market, which is a huge outdoor market where they sell everything on the street. Grandma likes the fruits and vegetables you can buy there. "Aren't they gor-jus!" she said.

We spent the whole day out. We saw a movie; we went to a science museum; we shopped in Eaton's, which is a huge department store. They have everything there. My favorite place in Eaton's, though, is the fountain on the lower level. The fountain snorts, spurts, then the water jets up. It's so pretty.

Every time I go to Toronto, Grandma and I go to Eaton's at least once to shop. When we get tired, we go downstairs and sit on the rim of the fountain and share a mini-baguette.

It's another one of our traditions. "We do this every year, Grandma."

"We'll do it next year, too, and the year after and the year after."

"We'll do it forever," I said.

Grandma passed me the last bit of crust. "I don't know how we did so much today, Bunny. We're just wonderful."

"Are you tired? Do you want to go home?"

"Oh, no, we're not through yet."

We ate supper in Grandma's favorite Japanese restaurant. Besides the regular tables, there were little booths with the tables in a well, so you could either put your legs and feet down or sit the way the Japanese people do. I was going to put my legs into the well, but after I saw Grandma sitting back on her heels like a Japanese woman, I sat that way, too.

"If more people ate the way the Japanese do, there wouldn't be so many overweights roaming the streets," Grandma said.

"Mmm." I liked the food, but there wasn't enough of it for me.

Grandma kept talking about how slim and trim and in shape Japanese people were, and how Westerners had so much to learn from them.

While she was in the middle of this, two women took the table across from us. They looked Japanese. They were both wearing suits and frilly blouses, high-heeled shoes, and hats. And they were definitely not slim and trim. They were plump and pretty.

Grandma cleared her throat and raised her eyebrows. "There's an exception to every rule, Bunny."

"Yeah, Grandma. Tell me about it."

The two women were talking in Japanese, and when the waitress came, they ordered their food in Japanese.

"Such an interesting language," Grandma said. "I wonder if it's difficult to learn."

When their food came, one dish after another, it looked like they'd ordered about ten times as much food as Grandma and me. The whole table was covered. "Oh, my!" one of them said. "This is gor-jus!" She sounded exactly like Grandma.

When we got home, Grandma took a shower and I went into the bedroom to pack my suitcase. But, instead, I sat down on Grandma's bed and called Emily.

First her mother answered. "Are you home, Bunny?" she said. "Emily will be so. . . . Let me call her! Emily! Guess who's. . . ."

Then Emily got on the phone. "Bunny? Where are you?"

"In Toronto."

"Why are you calling me? Aren't you coming home tomorrow?"

"My beloved, I couldn't go another day without talking to you."

"Yup. It's Bunny."

"Did the twins have a good party?"

"Yeah, we took them to Burger King. They each got a crown, the works. They loved it. Is that why you called?"

"Em. Remember James?"

"El gorgeous male?"

"Yes," I said. "Em." I cleared my throat. "I have something to tell you."

"You're madly in love with him," she said.

"That, too."

She thought I was joking. "And what else, Bunny?"

"Em . . . this is sort of weird, but. . . ." I cleared my throat again. "Well, I told him my name was Emily."

There was a silence. It seemed long to me.

Then Emily said, "What?"

"I told him my name was Emily," I repeated.

"That's what I thought you said. Why'd you do that?"

"Are you mad?"

"I'm — I don't know. I'm confused. You told him your name was my name?"

"It just seemed . . . better," I said.

"Oh," she said.

I sat on the edge of the bed and picked at the bedspread. "Em, it's not a big crime."

"No, it's just stupid. I'm just having trouble believing you did it."

"Okay, okay, get it all off your chest. I did it, I did a stupid thing, if that's what you think."

"Yeah, it is what I think, Bunny."

"Great. Thanks a lot." I hung up the phone.

Chapter 11

I didn't call Emily when I got home, and she didn't call me. And the next day in school, I didn't see her all morning. But at lunchtime, I walked over to our usual meeting place by the trophy case on the first floor. She was there. First we just looked at each other from opposite sides of the trophy case.

"Hi," I said.

"Hi," she said.

"Well, you look the same." She was wearing that green sweater.

"New jump suit?"

"Yeah. Grandma bought it for me in Eaton's."

"Uh huh."

"You like it?"

"It's nice."

We were being so polite! And we were still looking at each other over the trophy case. Then, suddenly, without either of us saying anything, but at the same moment, we ran toward each other and hugged.

Then we went outside to sit on the steps. We ate our lunches and talked, telling each other everything that had happened over the vacation. We kept interrupting each other and laughing and saying things like, "You should have been there! . . . You should have been with me."

Finally, I said, "Still mad at me for using your name?"

I guess I sounded a little anxious. I *was* a little anxious. I think when you love somebody and you have a fight and then make up, you feel so happy to be made up, it's like you love that person ten times more than you ever did. And you definitely don't want her to be mad at you for *anything*.

Emily linked her arm through mine. "No, I'm not mad. Can't you tell?" She passed me half her apple. "My father called me last night."

"There's somebody else you were mad at."

"I'm not mad at anybody, Bunny. I don't get mad that much."

"Tell me about it. What'd your father say?"

"Now he says he wants me to come visit this summer. Me and the twins at the same time. You know what that means, Bunny?" Her freckles were standing out all over her nose. "It means I'll get stuck taking care of Wilma and Chris, as usual! Plus my other baby sister. I don't mind taking care of her. I love her. But — free baby-sitting. . . . That's what Dad wants." She pressed her lips together.

I tapped her foot with mine. "Now that we're

all made up, I can't stand seeing you look so depressed."

She looked away from me.

"Emily! Cheer up!"

"Shut up," she said. "Don't. Don't do that — *Emily*," she added.

The way she said that made me jerk my arm out of hers. It came out of her mouth so scornful and sarcastic. "So sorry!" I said in my own sarcastic way.

Then we just sat there, each of us looking in another direction. Some reunion, I thought. Okay, I said a dumb thing. Did Emily have to get that nasty tone in her voice? And every time I did something the least bit wrong, was she going to remind me that I'd used her name?

"You can't make somebody cheer up by ordering them to do it, Bunny," she said.

"I know that!"

"Then why did you say it?"

"Emily, sometimes I just say things."

"Obviously! Like you said my name."

"I knew you were still mad at me about that."

She bent her head down onto her knees. After a moment she said, "No, I'm not, Bunny. I'm sorry. I'm just being mean because I feel so bad about my father. I don't think he loves me anymore. I really don't."

I put my arm around her. "Em? Let's start over again. You just said your father only wants you for a baby-sitter. And you got sort of depressed. And this time I didn't say anything, because I know what you mean. Okay?"

"Okay."

"Only I'm thinking something I want to tell you. I'm thinking it *sounds* that way about your father, but it doesn't have to *be* that way."

"Yes, it does." She still had her head down. "If I want to see him, what am I supposed to do?"

I didn't really know, I was just talking, trying to make Emily feel better. But then I remembered what my grandmother had said to me about taking a stand. At the time, I couldn't figure out why she said it, but now I thought, Maybe she had some kind of ESP. Maybe she knew — I don't mean actually, literally knew, but with some extra, different senses — that I would need that piece of advice.

"Emily, you know what I think?"

"What?"

"If you want something, you have to take a stand."

"Meaning?" She turned and looked up at me.

I've heard my dad talk about counseling people, about saying what you want, stuff like that, a million times. I just pulled it right out of my head. "Tell your father what you want. Just be clear in your own mind, then tell him. Like, if you don't want to go at the same time as the twins, you tell him that."

"I can't do that, Bunny."

"Yes, you can."

"It's hard to say something like that to your father. I don't want to hurt his feelings," she said anxiously.

"Yeah. I know what you mean. But you still have to do it. He's hurting your feelings."

"Do you really think I could just tell him?"

"You could try. What's he going to do? He could

say, No, you have to come at the same time as Wilma and Chris. Or he could say, Yeah! Why didn't I think of that?"

"Maybe I could write him a letter and say it. Or maybe a phone call would be easier. What do you think?"

"If it was me, I would write a letter. And then I would call him. I would do both."

We got up to go inside. Emily linked her arm with mine. "You're as good as Ann Landers."

"I'm better, because I tell jokes, too. If you put three ducks in a crate, what do you have?"

"Bunny, I know all your jokes by now! A box of quackers."

"Try this one. Did you hear about my aunt? Her name is Hortense Q. Story. She got married to Wappinger X. Short. Oh, I forgot to say, Aunt Hortense is seven feet tall. Poor dear. She had so much trouble finding clothes to fit her. But after she married Wappinger X. Short, she never had such trouble again."

"Why?" Emily said.

I tried not to smile. "Because getting married was a way of making a long story short."

"A long story — " Emily began, then she got it.

When I got home from school that day, there was a letter for me in the mail.

Dear B. Larrabee,

I'm pleased you ennoyed (that's what it said) *reading my book* Paris Plus. *I don't know the name of the young man on the cover. A professional model, I would assume.*

As to the more important question you ask, about in-spriation (maybe his typewriter couldn't spell), there may be such a thing, but it's a mistake to depend on it. If you want to be a comedian or a piano player or a modle (modle?) or a basketball star, work at it. Don't look for miracles.

Yours sincerely,

H. Diment

As soon as I read it, I called Emily. Wilma answered the phone. "You can't talk to Emily now, Bunny. She's in the toilet."

"Wilma, you don't have to say that."

"Why?"

"You could just tell me she's busy."

"Why?"

"Well, suppose I was somebody else calling."

"Who?"

"I don't know who, Wilma. I'm trying to get a point across. You know me, but you don't know everybody who calls. You don't tell people on the phone everything."

"Why?"

"Because I say so, Wilma. Get Emily, will you?"

"You can't talk to her now. She's in the — "

"Wilma! Just tell Emily to call me back later."

I went upstairs and fooled around with Shad and his animals for a while. Then Mom came home and she was frazzled. That's what she says the minute she walks in the house when she's had a hard day. "I'm frazzled!" She yells it, actually. Two or three times. "I'm frazzled! Frazzled! Frazzled!"

I was in the kitchen helping her make supper

when Emily called back. "Hi, Bunny. I was busy. I couldn't call you before."

"Em, you'll never guess. I have something big to tell you."

"Me, too. Bunny, *you'll* never guess — I called my father and told him."

"You told him?"

"Yes. Just what we talked about."

"You didn't!"

"I did! I really did it. I just this minute got off the phone. I yelled at him, Bunny. I got so upset, I just yelled and said, 'Dad, that's not fair! I shouldn't have to take care of kids on my vacation, too.' "

"What'd he say? Are you glad you did it? Was he mad? Tell me everything."

"He said he didn't expect me to take care of the kids. He kept saying that I was coming to visit him and Marcia, that it was a visit and a vacation and I would have fun. I think that's what he said. I'm sort of dazed. I don't even believe yet I did it."

"You did it! You really did it. I'm proud of you."

"Me, too," Emily said. She really did sound proud of herself.

"Get off the phone, Bunny," Mom said. "Call Emily back later. I need your help now."

"Mom, I just have to talk to Emily for a few minutes more. Em — "

"Later," Mom said.

"Mom, five minutes — "

"You've already had ten minutes. I need your help NOW," Mom said.

"What about Shad?"

"Bunny. Hang. Up. That. Phone."

I hung up.

"And don't sulk," Mom said.

"I'm not sulking! Shad," I yelled, "you come down here and help."

"What're you yelling about?" Shad said, walking in.

Mom stuck a broom in his hand. "Sweep. Bunny, get out the frozen peas. Then start the salad."

"Sorry you're not still at Grandma's?" Shad said, sweeping around my feet.

"Believe it. This family is the worst."

Dad came in a few minutes later. He had bought a frozen dessert. "Chocolate mouse," Mom said. "I need something to make me feel better. I had a hard day and your daughter is giving me a hard time." She gave Dad a kiss.

"Mousse," Dad said. "Not mouse. Chocolate mousse."

Mom pulled the dinner plates out of the cupboard. "Mooose. Mouse. What's the difference? You don't have to always correct me. There are certain words that I get mixed up. So what?"

"They're not that hard to remember, Lorraine."

"For me, they are. Especially today. I'm frazzled! So I get confused between the fish — which is spelled B-A-S-S — and the singing voice — which, for some reason I've never been able to understand, is also spelled B-A-S-S — and so what?"

"Mom, you just have to remember the fish is bass, like basketball," Shad said, "and the voice is bass, like baseball."

"I don't think that helps at all," Mom said.

"Even Shad knows," Dad said.

"What do you mean, *even*?" Shad complained.

"Okay, my kid is smarter than me," Mom said.

"That's all I need today! So I make a mistake. Do you have to correct me? Let me mispronounce stuff. Let me be not perfect, which is myself. Let me be a little goofy!"

"Who can stop you?" Dad said.

In the middle of all that, the phone rang. "I'll get it." I thought it was Emily again. It's a good thing I answered. It was James.

"Hi, Emily," he said.

"Hi!"

"Who is it?" Dad said.

"Get off the phone," Mom said. "We're going to eat. Tell Emily to call you back."

"I can't talk right now," I said to James. "We're just sitting down to eat supper. Can I call you back later?"

"Sure."

"Okay. 'Bye."

" 'Bye," he said.

" 'Bye," I said. I waited until he hung up, and then I did. " 'Bye," I said, under my breath. " 'Bye, sweet James."

Chapter 12

Saturday, when I was ready to leave the house, my father asked, "Where are you going?"

"To the mall."

"Who are you going with?"

"Emily."

"What are you going to do there?"

"Dad! What do you do in the mall? Shop."

"Is that all?"

"Is that all what?"

"Is that all you're going to do?"

"She's returning a library book for me," Mom said.

"And I'm going to buy that special toothpaste for you, Dad." He has sensitive gums. I held up the list Mom had given me. "Okay? Can I leave now?"

"Have enough money?" he asked. He gave me a couple of dollars and I left.

As soon as I walked out the door, I felt better. The whole time Dad was asking me questions, I felt bad. I always feel that way when I'm lying. Not that I was actually saying anything *un*true, but there was something I wasn't saying. Which was that besides shopping in the mall, I was also going to meet James.

But first I met Emily at the south entrance. I had bought a bag of almonds on the way over. "Want some?" I asked, holding out the little white bag to her.

"No, thanks, I don't like almonds."

"You don't? They're my favorite nut."

"Not mine. My favorite nut — "

" — is me," I said quickly. I gave her a wrinkly grin.

"Beep. Beep. *Beep! Baaad* joke alert." We went up on the escalator. "I thought so," Emily said. "You're nervous."

"Me? I am not. Why do you say that?"

"You're humming. You always hum when you're nervous."

"I do? Since when?"

"Since always," Emily said firmly. "Don't you know that about yourself?"

We got off the escalator and walked over toward the Häagan-Dazs ice-cream stand and got in line.

"You want raspberry, as usual?" Emily asked.

"Sure." She ordered and got us napkins and took out her change purse to pay. I remembered how I'd paid for James's gelato when I met him the first time. And I thought about him, about seeing him again. In just a little bit over an hour, I'd be sitting opposite him at the same table, where we sat before.

When I'd called him back Monday night, we'd agreed to meet today. "Same place, same time," James had said. "I'll bring a copy of the newspaper with *the* article to show you, Emily. Plus, I owe you a gelato. Right?"

I hummed under my breath. Was I nervous? I didn't think so. Then, I heard myself humming. "Emily, I'll never be able to hum again without thinking it means I'm a nervous wreck. Even if I'm not."

"Well, I wouldn't blame you if you were," she said. She took the two ice-cream cones and handed me mine. "I would be, if I were you."

"Why? I'm not meeting Jack the Ripper."

"No, but he is a stranger, Bunny."

"He is not."

"You've only talked to him on the phone two times — "

"Three times, Emily."

"Okay, three times. Big deal."

"Plus, I've met him in person. At this very gelato place where I'm going to meet him today. And nothing horrendous happened to me. As you can see."

"I'm sorry, maybe I'm just a worrywart type. You didn't tell me the first time you met him — "

"I told you, it was spur of the moment. It wasn't something we planned."

"— or I would have been ten times more worried than I am now."

"Then I'm glad I didn't tell you, Emily. What

good is worrying, anyway? I mean, if something is going to happen to me, it's going to happen, right?"

"That's ridiculous. Are you just giving up control over yourself?" She flung out her arms and lolled her head back on her neck. "What's going to happen is going to happen," she said, with an utterly dopey expression.

"I didn't mean that." I was so annoyed I pinched her.

So she pinched me back, but harder. "I just want you to be careful."

"Okay. Okay. Okay. O. Kay. I will be careful. Feel better now?"

"I know you think I'm too cautious."

"I never said that."

"You're the daring one."

"Emily, what's so daring about me?"

"Well, this whole thing with James. It's an adventure. I wouldn't have had the nerve to go through with it. I probably wouldn't even have talked to your James the first time."

"*My* James," I said. "My, my!" But I liked that. All the time we were doing our shopping, that little phrase went round and round in my head. *My James.*

We did our shopping. Every time I threw something else into my shopping bag, I'd check my watch.

At five minutes before four, I said, "I'm going over now, Em. I'll call you later and tell you all about it."

"I think I'll go with you," Emily said.

"What do you mean? You can't."

94

"Why not? I want to be sure that everything's okay. You can just say your friend came with you."

"Emily, I don't want to say that. Anyway, it's a terrible idea. How am I supposed to introduce you? Emily? *My* name is Emily, remember?"

"You could just tell him Emily's not your name, and — "

"No way, José! He'll think I'm a complete space cadet. What do I say? Oh, sorry, James, the first time I met you, I had a little slip of the mind and I just happened to give you the wrong name. The real Emily is right here, while the other Emily, meaning me, is actually Bunny."

"Well, you could say it. What's so bad about that?"

"Emily, I'm not going to do it."

"Bunny — "

"And *please* don't call me that right now. What if he's here already?" The minute I said it, I had to turn around and look. I sneaked another glance at my watch. "Why did you have to spring this on me?" I said. "We could have figured something out, but it's too late now."

Again I got that same bad feeling I had when I was fibbing to my father. The truth was, I didn't want to figure anything out. I didn't want Emily there when I met James. As soon as I thought that, I felt sort of panicky and almost sick. What was happening? Was our friendship falling apart? I'd *always* wanted Emily *everywhere* with me. I couldn't think of another time in my life when I didn't want her to be with me or do something with me. Not one single time.

"Bun — " Emily took my arm. "Okay, what if I

don't sit with you? I could just go in by myself and take a table, and — "

"No."

"Why not?"

"I don't want you to do that."

"Why not?"

"Because I *said* I don't want you to."

"Why not?"

"You're starting to sound like Wilma."

"Look, Bun — look, I won't talk to you. I'll just sit there and — "

"*No.* Why are you so worried about me? What do you think I'm going to do? Throw myself at his feet? Run away with him?" Didn't anybody trust me? First my father. *Where are you going? What are you doing? Who are you doing it with?* Now Emily and her nervous hovering.

"I don't want you *lurking*, Emily. I don't want you spying on me. I don't want you protecting me." I was mad. I let myself get mad, and I was *glad* to be mad, because then I didn't have to think about the way I was acting.

"I'm not going to spy, Bunny! What a horrible thing to say. I just want to be there as — as insurance."

"And I don't want you there as an insurance policy, either. Just have some faith in me. I'm not a complete airhead."

"No, but if you weren't so busy thinking about yourself — "

"Oh, yes, I know! I know! I'm selfish and insensitive."

We stopped in the middle of the mall. People

hurried around us. Somebody's shopping bag slapped into my back.

"Bunny, if you'd just listen for a moment. I — "

"I am listening, and I don't like what I hear. And don't call me Bunny."

" — want to see him, too. Did that ever occur to you? First you talk about him and talk about him, and then you tell me I can't even see him. When am *I* going to see him?"

"Okay, you can walk by and take a quick look."

"I can walk by and take a quick look? Thank you so much! Thank you, thank you, your majesty. Or should I call you Generalissimo? You like power, don't you?"

"Me?"

"Yes! You enjoy pushing people around."

"Oh! How nasty!" At that point, I was so mad I didn't care who heard us. James could have walked right up to us and I wouldn't have been able to stop. "You talk about me, Emily. You have a queen bee complex. You're so used to bossing poor little Wilma and Chris, lording it over them, that it's a habit now. You're just mad because you can't boss me around, too."

Emily's face was pale. Her freckles practically jumped off her skin. "Talk about nasty. You are the expert. You know more about it than anybody."

She walked away from me.

Chapter 13

I went around the corner to Stanchio's. I went in and sat down at a table. The place was empty. There was music playing. A man was singing. *"To tell you the truth, girl, I'm madly . . . badly . . . in love with youuuuuu. . . ."*

"I'm waiting for a friend," I told the man behind the counter. The same man with the bald, freckled head. He nodded.

My stomach was jumping around from the fight with Emily. I tapped my fingers on the table. When the song was done, it started playing over again. The man behind the counter said, "That's one of my favorite songs. You know what I do?"

I shook my head.

"Every day I play just one song in the morning and one song in the afternoon. I listen to the song playing over and over, and that's the way I learn the lyrics."

"That's very interesting," I said politely.

"To tell you the truth, girl, I'm madly . . . badly . . . in love with youuuuuu. . . ." I was sitting with my back to the window. All of a sudden, I got this feeling that somebody was watching me. Eyes on my back. *Emily*, I thought. She's right out there, spying on me, making sure I don't do anything dumb.

I turned around. Somebody was watching me, all right. James. He waved and came in. "Hi. Did you just get here?" He sat down across from me.

"I've been shopping."

"Buy anything good?"

"Toothpaste."

The counterman brought water. "We have good tortelloni. I made them myself this morning fresh."

"That sounds good," James said. "How about you, Emily?"

"Raspberry — no, vanilla-rum gelato."

"Coming up," the man said.

James took a drink of water. "Well, I finally got that story written. And published." He took a small, folded newspaper out of his hip pocket.

I leaned forward. "Can I see it?"

"I'm sorta nervous about showing you. I hope you think it's good."

"Of course I will." I reached for the paper, but before I even looked at it, I thought of something. "Did you use my name?"

James shook his head. "No, you'll see. I was going to, then I decided it would be better not to. I hope you're not disappointed."

"Oh, that's okay." I was relieved! I don't know

why, but the idea of *my* memory with Emily's name on it seemed, well, dishonest. Maybe that doesn't make sense. Because I didn't think it was dishonest to use Emily's name. Or maybe it does make sense. Because I didn't like my name, but I liked my memories.

"It's on the inside page," he said.

"To tell you the truth, girl, I'm madly . . . badly . . . in love with youuuuuu. . . ."

I opened the paper and spread it out on the table. The headline said: LULU BELLE WOWS DEVOTED FANS. And underneath, it began: *"A mob of screaming, singing, cheering fans greeted Lulu Belle and her band at the Civic Center last week. I was there in the spirit of curiosity — who were the people who grooved on this music? — and helpfulness. Your intrepid Teen Seen Reporter, Maureen Flint, roped me into this deal.*

" 'I can't go,' she said. 'I need someone to fill in for me. You're a friend. Prove it.' Since Maureen is always saying this sort of thing to me with a suspicious glint in her eye, I thought, Okay, I'll do it! This will be the supreme test. What better way to prove my friendship than to sit through an entire evening of Lulu Belle Smith?"

I read down to the end of the article. It was really good. I thought maybe he'd pretend to have interviewed a lot of people, but he didn't. He just wrote about me, some of the things I told him about how much I liked Lulu Belle's music and why.

"So what do you think?" he said.

I folded the newspaper again. "It's really good."

"You like it? You really do? Maureen thought you'd have a fit, because I didn't use your name.

She says most people want to see their names in print."

"No. I'm glad you didn't."

"You never have that yen? You don't want to see your name in a newspaper?"

"Well, maybe, some day." A headline flashed into my mind. COMEDY SENSATION STARTS NEW TV SEASON WITH OWN SHOW. RISES TO THE TOP FROM HUMBLE BEGINNING UNDER BIG TOP.

James leaned across the table toward me. "So, anyway, you made your contribution to my short career as a reporter."

"Right, now you go full steam ahead for law."

"Uh huh. What about you?"

"Didn't I tell you? I'm going to be a clown."

"I never knew a girl who did that."

Under the table, James's legs twined around mine. My face heated up. I started to burn. Even my eyelids got hot. "I'll probably go to clown college." My voice sounded like a robot's.

"A clown in college. That's cute."

My legs were trapped inside his legs. I couldn't stop blushing. "What do you mean, cute"?

"Cute. It's cute. You'd make a cute clown. Emily, the cute clown."

"It's not *cute*," I said. That annoyed me, and I was still blushing. "I'm serious. I think it's my life's calling."

"Your life's calling!"

"Do you think it's *cute* that you want to be a lawyer?"

"Sure I do. Do you think I'm being sexist?" Everything I said amused him.

"James!"

"Em-ily!"

"Why do you laugh at me?"

"I told you. You're cute and adorable." He leaned even closer and kissed me. After the first moment of shock, I closed my eyes. I thought, *I better remember this.* My eyes were still closed when James pulled away. For a moment I didn't want to open them. At all. Ever.

Then the counterman was standing over our table, putting the tortelloni with cream sauce in front of James and the gelato in front of me. "Enjoy," he said.

And I heard the song again, the same words, the same chorus. *"To tell you the truth, girl, I'm madly . . . badly . . . in love with youuuuuu. . . ."*

I ran through the mall, looking for Emily. I don't know how long I ran around, trying to find her. It never even occurred to me that she might not be there, that she might have gone home. I went in and out of stores and I finally saw her near Jeans An' Things. "Emily! Emily!" I grabbed her by the shoulder. "Emily, wait till you hear — "

"Excuse *me!*" the woman said. She was small and dark-haired like Emily, and cute from the back in her jeans, but from the front she was definitely not Emily. She had a little peaky, pointed face with a bright red nose.

"Oh, sorry," I said. "I thought you were — "

"I'm not," she said, in a loud voice. She looked furious. "Rude, badly brought up kids!"

"Sorry," I said again. "Really."

I kept on looking for Emily and I found her, too,

after I'd made a big circle, in the bookstore across from the gelato shop. "Hi, Em."

She turned around. "I'm not lurking," she said, right away. "I'm looking for a book for Wilma."

I dragged her out of the store and told her everything.

"He put his legs around your legs?" she said.

"Yes!"

"He kissed you?"

"Yes!"

She squeezed her hands together. "What did you do?"

"Nothing. I closed my eyes."

"You closed your eyes? And then what?"

"I thought, I'm going to remember this until the day I die."

"Was it wonderful?"

"It was strange."

"It was strange? Why?"

"Well . . . maybe because he just, um, *did* it. Here we were — talking . . . and all of a sudden, he leans across the table and smacks his lips on mine."

"*Smacks* his lips?" Emily said. "Yuuck."

"No, no, I said that wrong. I just meant that, you know, we were talking and all of a sudden, he did it, there were his lips, stuck on my lips."

"Okay, so then what happened?"

"My gelato and his tortelloni came. No, I'm not kidding. It did."

"And then?"

"And then we stopped kissing, and we ate, and we talked some more."

"How did you feel?"

"Emily." I linked my arm with hers and talked right into her ear. "That gelato tasted *so good*. It was cold. Oh, it was so good. My lips were burning, I mean it, they were just burning up — do they look burning now?"

She inspected me and shook her head. "No, they look fine. They look normal."

"It's a good thing. I wouldn't want to go home with fat, burning lips."

"What'd you talk about? Did you talk about the kiss?"

"We never mentioned it. It was funny, because that was about ninety percent of what I was thinking about. Or maybe ninety-five percent. Anyway, I told him how old I was."

"You told him how old you were?"

"Emily, you're repeating everything I say."

"I'm repeating everything you say?"

"There! You're doing it again."

"Did you tell him about your name, too?"

"Hey. One big truth a day is enough for me."

We sat down under the skylight at one of the little Cinzano tables with umbrellas. "Bunny," Emily said, "did you really tell him you were thirteen?"

I nodded. "It just came out. I didn't know I was going to say it. First he kissed me. Then the gelato came. My gelato. And his tortelloni. He started eating. He said, 'Aren't you going to eat your gelato?' So I did for a while, just cooling my lips. And then I looked at him and I said, 'James. I'm thirteen years old.' "

The minute I repeated it to Emily, my face got

hot and I remembered the way James had leaned across the table and kissed me.

"You said it just like that?"

I held up my right hand. "Girl Scout's honor."

"What did he do? What did he say?"

"He said he was astonished. I'm quoting. That's exactly what he said. *I'm astonished.*'"

"He didn't know you were thirteen?"

"No. He's eighteen, Emily. Remember I said he might be even eighteen? He is. He just had his birthday last month. He said he thought I was at least fifteen, maybe even sixteen."

"Okay. And then what?"

"I don't know. We just talked some more and then he paid for the gelato and stuff, and we got up and left."

"Are you going to see him again?"

"I don't know. I don't think so. The article's all done. I don't think he'll call me again. Do you?"

"How do I know? I never even met the guy! I never even *saw* him. In fact, I'm still mad at you," she said, pulling away her arm.

"No, you're not." I took her arm and put it through mine again. "You can't still be mad at me, because I'm not mad at you anymore."

"Bunny — "

"Em-ily." The moment I said that, I remembered how James had said the same thing to me, and I felt a pang or a pain, some kind of queer, hard, tightening feeling in my chest. And I thought, Bunny, why did you have to tell him your age? Why did you have to do that?

Chapter 14

Monday night, after supper, Shad and I were watching tv in his room when the phone rang.

"I'm going to take a shower," Mom called from the hall. "Somebody else answer that."

"Get it, Bunny," Shad said. He was lying on his belly on the floor.

"Nobody's going to call me."

"How about Emily?"

The phone rang again. "It's probably for Dad," I said.

"Nobody ever calls him."

"What about his clients?"

"Only the crazy ones call."

"Shad, you better not let Dad hear you say that."

The phone rang for the third time. I jumped up and ran across the hall to Mom and Dad's room. I picked up the phone, just in time to hear Dad saying, "There's no Emily here."

"Dad, I'll take it," I said.

"Emily?" James said.

"Just a minute. Dad? Are you off the phone? This is personal."

I heard the phone click downstairs.

"Hi," I said. I sat down on the bed. I'd been thinking about James practically every single moment since Saturday. And I dreamed about him, too.

I dreamed that we were in an airplane together. I was flying the plane, and James was sitting there, with his legs crossed, wearing a pair of shorts.

"Was that your father?" he said.

"Yeah. He thought I wasn't home," I said quickly.

"Well, I'm glad you were. I wanted to talk to you. You know, I was talking about you to Maureen and — "

"You were talking about me to Maureen? Why?"

"Oh, interesting case."

My face got red. "What?"

"No, don't get mad. I was just telling her about you. Don't worry. All good things. And, anyway — were you kidding when you said you were thirteen?"

I didn't answer right away. What if I said, Yes. Sure, I was kidding. It was all a joke. One of my big jokes. I'd tell James he'd been right. I was really fifteen. No, sixteen.

And he'd say, Whew! Terrific! Because, to tell you the truth, girl, I'm madly in love with you.

"I'm thirteen," I said. "Well, almost fourteen. My birthday is in August."

"Three more months," he said. "But that's still sorta young."

"For what?" I blurted.

"For me. Well, maybe I'll see you when you're a little older. Bye-bye, little girl."

Little girl. My face got as hot as when he kissed me. "I don't appreciate that," I said. "I don't think that's a very nice thing to say."

"No, I didn't mean — Well . . . sorry about that. But, you know, it's the truth."

"I'm not — " I had to pause and take in a big breath of air. I didn't like that! I didn't like being called a little girl. Why did he have to say it? Just because he was older than me? "That's kind of shallow thinking, isn't it? I mean, just because of someone's age, suddenly not liking them?"

"You've got it wrong. I do like you. I just meant — you know, you're too young for me."

"I'm not a little girl," I said. "And you didn't think that until you knew my age. That's what I mean about shallow." I didn't know I was going to say all that. If you'd asked me before James called, I would have said if I had another chance to talk to him, I'd be as sweet and nice and charming and lovable as I knew how to be.

"Emily?" he said. "Let's say good-bye as friends. Are you willing?"

I nodded, as if he could see me. "Okay."

" 'Bye, Emily," he said. His voice was so sweet! "It was fun knowing you."

" 'Bye, James," I said. I hung up and then I just sat on the bed for a while. I was almost crying.

I heard Dad come up the steps. "Off the phone, Bunny?" He came into the room.

"Yes."

"Who was that?"

"A boy."

"Uh huh. Somebody from school?"

"No."

"Where do you know him from?"

"What?" I was still sort of dazed.

"Where do you know him from?" he said again.

"Where do I know James from?"

"Is that his name? James?"

I nodded.

"So?" Dad said. He sounded very patient.

"What?"

"Where do you know him from, honey?"

"Oh. The concert. The Lulu Belle concert."

"Didn't he ask for Emily?"

"I guess so."

"He did. He asked for Emily. Why is that, Bunny?"

"Dad, it's okay. There's nothing to worry about."

Mom came in from the bathroom in her red robe. Her hair was wound up in a towel. "What's going on?"

"Dad is worried that I'm doing something dumb. Or growing up too fast. Or something."

"Dad is not worried," Dad said. "Dad is just waiting to hear about this somewhat unusual situation. Some young man just called her," he said to Mom, "and asked for Emily."

"Emily?" Mom said. "Is he a friend of Emily's, Bunny?"

I got up and then I sat down again. Mom sat down next to me on the bed and started toweling her hair. Dad leaned against the bureau, smoking.

"Remember when I went to the concert?" They both nodded. "Well . . . I met this guy there. He was sitting next to me and we started talking. He was going to write an article about the concert, and he interviewed me."

"Okay," Dad said. "And — ?"

"And — so that was fun. I liked being interviewed."

Mom came out from under her towel to say, "Yeah, I liked it, too, when the newspaper did that piece on Officer Friendly last year. Remember?"

"But he just called you now," Dad said. "The concert was quite a while ago."

"Well, he called me before this, too. And I met him a couple of times." I shrugged.

"Met him where?" Mom said.

"Gelato place in the mall."

"Oh. Well, that's a good place to meet. Good and public."

"Wait, I have a feeling there's something more," Dad said.

"More, like what?" I was thinking of the kiss. I didn't want to talk about that. No, I wouldn't.

"Well, for one thing, what's this about Emily? How does she figure in it?"

My face heated up. I have to admit I felt a little ashamed to tell them. I mean, it's one thing to complain about my name to Mom, which I do all the time, and another thing to come right out and admit that I think it's such a crummy name I don't even want to tell it to a guy I like.

"Why did he ask for Emily?" Dad said. "Is he a friend of hers?"

I shook my head.

"She didn't even go to the concert with you, did she?"

"No," Mom said. "She did not. Bunny?"

The way she said it, I knew I had to tell her. Mom goes along and goes along and then she hits a point where you don't fool around with her.

I sighed. "He told me his name. And then he asked me my name, and I don't know why, I mean I didn't plan it, but I said my name was Emily."

"You what?"

I had to repeat it. "I said my name was Emily."

They both looked at me like I was certifiable. "You used Emily's name? Why? What was the point?"

"I guess I didn't want to use my name."

"So you got yourself into a little bit of a bind?" Mom said.

"Yeah."

She put her arm around me. "Come on, that doesn't seem so terrible. It's not what I would recommend for the beginning of a friendship, but it's not world-class crime, either."

I sighed again. "Well, he thinks my name is Emily. And once I said it, it was like, How do I undo this? I couldn't! It just got to the point where *I* began to think of myself as being named Emily every time I talked to him."

"I can imagine." Mom was really nice about it. But Dad was still giving me his look — not a mean look, just that sort of soft, thoughtful look that means he's got something on his mind and any minute now, you're going to find out what it is.

"How old did you say this boy is?" Dad said.

"I didn't." How did he know to go to that? That's what I mean about thoughtful looks.

"How old is he?" Dad said.

"A little bit older than I am."

"How old is that?" Mom said.

"Um. A few years. Actually, he's eighteen."

"Eighteen!" Mom said. She and Dad looked at each other.

"Mom, it's okay," I said quickly. "We're not even going to see each other again."

"Again?" she said. "You have seen each other?"

"Yeah, I told you. Two times, in the gelato place."

"Two times?"

She sounded like Emily, repeating everything I said.

"Right."

"Well, what did you do there?"

"Mom, what do you think? We ate gelato. Well, the second time, I had gelato and he had tortelloni."

Mom started laughing. "Oh, Bunny!"

"Come on, Lorraine," Dad said. "That's no help."

"Sorry," Mom said. She hid her face in her hands for a moment. "Okay, okay, this is serious. Sweetie — " She looked at me. "I mean this. I'm not fooling around. This boy is too old for you. I don't want you — Dad and I do not approve of your seeing an eighteen-year-old boy."

"I know."

"He could be the nicest boy in the world, but he's definitely too old for you. Eighteen and thirteen just don't mix. Or if they do, they shouldn't."

"I know," I said again. "I told you, we're not going to see each other anymore." Every time I said it, I felt bad. No, I didn't. I felt terrible.

Chapter 15

A few days later, at supper, Mom mentioned that her boss wanted her to go to Toronto over the weekend. There was going to be a convention of people who worked in police public relations departments. "People will be coming from all over the United States and Canada. It's a great opportunity for me. I'll drive up late Friday afternoon and — "

"You can't go," Dad interrupted. "I'm going to San Diego Friday morning. Don't you remember? I won't be back until Tuesday night."

"You didn't tell me you were going to San Diego," Shad said. He fed Benjie, who was in his pocket, a piece of bread. "Nobody tells me anything."

"Well, I have to go to Toronto," Mom said. "This is important. My boss thinks — "

"If it's so important, why did they just tell you about it now?" Dad said. "What kind of planning is that? What if you had other plans already made?"

"I don't. I kept this weekend open. I more or less knew about it a couple of months ago, but my boss wasn't sure if he could get an okay for funding. You know how the budget is. They're paying my transportation and food. As it is, I told them I'd stay at Mother's."

"Excellent, but who's going to stay here, with the kids?"

"Well, I thought you were going to be here."

"I told you weeks ago about this convention," Dad said.

Mom looked upset. "I know, I remember now. I'm sorry, I just didn't keep it straight."

"You should have put it on your calendar."

"I know, you're right, but I never do those good, organized things. You know how I am."

"Nobody has to stay with me," I said. "I can take care of myself just fine."

"No, sweetie, you're not staying in the house alone," Mom said.

And Dad added, "Absolutely not. That's not even up for discussion."

What did they think I was going to do? Invite James and all his friends over for an orgy? "This family is so unfair," I said.

Mom looked at me. "Really?"

I hated the way she said that one little word. Like she didn't believe me at all.

"Yes, really."

"What does that mean?"

"Forget it, Mom!"

"I don't want to forget it, Bunny. What is this

stuff about unfairness? Don't you think you ought to tell Dad or me if you have a complaint?"

Mom gets this extremely reasonable tone of voice that is so irritating. It sounds as if she's always right, and I'm always wrong. "Well, I just said that nobody had to look after me. I could stay home this weekend. I'm not exactly a child, but neither you or Dad even considers it. I'm not even given a choice about things. It's just orders from on high. Orders from headquarters. Bunny, you are going to do this and this, and this and that, and that's *that*!"

"Well." My mother pushed her glasses up on her head. "Such vehemence. Did you and Emily have a fight?"

"Everybody always says that! As if that's the only thing in my world." It was so irritating. "Why don't you just admit you won't let me stay alone, because you don't trust me?"

"We do trust you," Mom said. "That's not true."

"Wait," Dad said. "Hold it. We can't go into this now. We still have to make a decision about the weekend."

"I know how we can do it," Mom said. "Bunny can come with me to Toronto. And Shad can go with you."

"Bunny just went to Toronto," Shad said. "That's not fair."

"Shad can't come with me," Dad said to Mom. "I'm sorry, honey, but there'll be nothing for him to do for three days. Besides, I doubt I could get him a ticket this late in the game."

Well, the end of all that was that Dad flew to

San Diego alone Friday morning, and Mom, Shad, and I drove up to Toronto together Friday afternoon.

It was past midnight by the time we got to Grandma's. She was still up, waiting for us. She hugged Shad, then me.

"Sure, your own daughter last," Mom said. "How are you, Mommy?"

They walked into the living room with their arms around each other. "Oh, you know me," Grandma said. "I have my little complaints, I had a pretty bad headache today, but I keep going."

Mom and Grandma slept in the twin beds. Shad had a sleeping bag on the floor, and I slept on the couch. The next morning, Mom had to go out early for her conference. She bent over me and whispered, "Sleep okay?"

I nodded and sat up.

Mom put her finger to her lips and looked over to where Shad was all rolled up in his sleeping bag. "Shad is still sawing wood. Why don't you try to get some more sleep, honey?"

"Okay. You look nice." She was wearing a plum-colored suit and a pale pink blouse.

"Thanks." She kissed me. She smelled of toothpaste. "I'll see you later."

I slept some more. Then I got up and Shad did, too. We went in the kitchen and got out the breakfast cereal. "I'm going to explore the city," Shad said.

"I'll give you my map. Do you want some cocoa?"

We were just sitting down when Grandma came

in. She was wearing jeans and a blue T-shirt that said YES, I CAN.

"Grandma! I never saw you in a T-shirt."

"Oh, yes, I wear them sometimes. It was so quiet here, I thought you two were still sleeping."

"We've been up for ages," I said.

"Grandma," Shad said, "I'm going to explore Toronto. I'll take Bunny's map."

Grandma sat down with her coffee. "Now, Shad, I'm all for independence, but this makes me a little nervous. I think I'd like you to confine yourself to the neighborhood."

"Grandma, I'm very capable."

"I know you are, darling, but if your mother takes off my head, it's my head, not yours." She lit a cigarette and blew smoke over her shoulder. "Shhh, both of you. Don't say anything about my cigarettes. I know all about it."

Shad put his dishes in the sink. "I'm going out, now."

"Not until you promise me you won't go too far," Grandma said. "Toronto is a good city, but it's not paradise."

"Grandma," I said, "I never thought I'd hear you say that."

Shad got his jacket. "I'll just go a few blocks." He looked at his wristwatch. "And I'll come back in an hour."

"Fair enough," Grandma said. He went out and Grandma and I sat at the table, talking.

She put her hand over mine. "This is wonderful. I thought I wouldn't see you for another year."

"Oh, no, I would have come back sooner.

Grandma, I have a problem with Mom."

"What's that, darling?"

I started to tell her about Mom not trusting me. "What I think doesn't count for anything. Supposing I didn't want to come up here and see you — I mean, just supposing — "

Grandma was leaning toward me, nodding as if she understood.

"I did, of course, but I could have stayed home. I'm going to be fourteen in three months. Don't you think that's old enough to stay home alone sometimes?"

Grandma lit another cigarette. She blew out the match and, as she did, she got this strange expression on her face. It was almost like a smile, but not quite. Her lips curled up, as if she'd just heard a joke, but a joke she didn't like at all.

Then her cigarette fell out of her hand and she slumped over. Her head hit the table, she said something, and fell off the chair.

Chapter 16

Grandma was lying on the floor, her arms crumpled under her and one of her legs caught in the rung of the chair. Her eyes stared up at me. "Grandma," I whispered. And then I shouted. "Grandma!" I bent over her. "Grandma, come on, get up." I put my hand under her shoulder. I couldn't move her. There was spit at the corner of her mouth.

Her eyes were staring at me, so I knew she wasn't dead. She lay on the floor. Nothing moved. I tried to straighten out her arms. Her eyes stared and stared. It looked like they were talking to me, trying to tell me something. I ran to the phone in her bedroom, then I ran back and bent over her. "Grandma, darling, don't worry, I'm calling Mom."

I stroked her hand. I stroked her hair. I didn't want to leave her. I went into the bedroom again. I couldn't think of the name of the hotel where

Mom's convention was being held. I sat on the bed, breathing hard. I put my hands around my face and squeezed my head. *Think, Bunny. Think.*

"Okay," I said out loud. I talked to myself. "You can call Mom after. Call the ambulance first. No, call the operator, she'll help you." I dialed the operator. The phone rang and rang. "Oh, hurry, please."

"Operator."

"I need an ambulance. My grandmother — I don't know what it is. I don't think it's a heart attack. She's on the floor, she — "

"I'll connect you with the emergency room of St. Michael's."

"Thank you." I heard myself being polite. I wanted to laugh. I thought, No, you can't do that. I noticed I wasn't crying. I noticed how calm my voice was. All sorts of things were going through my mind. It was as if there was another person inside me commenting on everything I was doing.

Good, Bunny, you called the operator, that was the right thing to do. Now the phone is ringing. Okay, now somebody's answering. It's the emergency room. Tell them what you told the operator. Right, now they want the address. Say it clearly, Bunny. That's good. You're doing fine.

I hung up. Mom. Where was she? I started looking in the phone directory under hotels. I went through them all. I was sure I would recognize the name of the hotel. Nothing looked familiar. The convention was at a hotel, wasn't it? Or was that Dad's convention? I couldn't remember.

I went back to Grandma. I got her leg untangled from the chair. Why hadn't I done that before? I wet a dish towel and wiped her face and sat down on the floor near her and put her head in my lap.

"Grandma." I talked to her. I told her I'd called the hospital and that the ambulance was coming. I wanted to say, Grandma, I'm scared. I kept stroking her hair. I didn't know what else to do.

The doorbell rang. "Maybe that's them right now." I put her head down on the floor again. That seemed horrible and I folded the dish towel under her head.

The doorbell rang and rang. Then someone knocked. I ran into the hall and opened the door. It was Shad. "It took you long enough," he said. "Can I go out again?"

"Shad." I pulled him into the foyer. "Shhh."

"Who's sleeping? Where's Grandma?"

"She's in the kitchen. Shad — "

"I've got to pee, then I want to go out again. Look." He pulled a Canadian dollar out of his pocket. "I got it in a store."

"Shad, shut up. Grandma's sick."

He frowned. "What do you mean, she's sick? Where is she?" He started toward the kitchen.

"Wait," I said.

He went into the kitchen and then backed out, knocking into me. Outside, I heard the ambulance siren. "What's the matter with Grandma?" He looked like he was going to cry.

"I don't know. She fell off her chair. I think it's a stroke." I didn't know I was going to say that. I didn't know that I knew that.

"Bunny, is she dead?"

"No. I think she can hear things. It's her eyes." I went over and knelt next to Grandma again.

"Grandma, they're coming. They're coming soon. Shad's here. See, he came right back, just the way he said he would." I kept talking to her.

It seemed so long since I'd phoned for the ambulance. It seemed like hours, but when the doorbell rang, I looked at the clock and I saw it was only fifteen minutes.

I opened the door. Two people in whites were there with a rolled-up stretcher. "Hello."

Why did they say hello? I didn't want them to be polite. I didn't care about manners or politeness. "My grandmother — she's in there." I pointed to the kitchen. They walked in. I wanted them to run. Everything they did seemed too slow and then it seemed too fast.

I watched them put Grandma onto the stretcher. Her eyes stared up. Now her eyes were talking to them. They put a blanket over her.

"Anybody else home?" the man asked.

"No. Just us."

"Don't worry, love," the woman said. She had an English accent. "We'll take good care of her."

"Can I go with you?"

They looked at each other. "Well, you know, it's just going to be sitting around the hospital all day. Where's your mum?"

"She's in a meeting at the convention center." The second time that happened to me. I said something I couldn't think of before.

"Well, does she know? Why don't you call there?"

"Yes, I'm going to."

"Then she can come home and go to the hospital with you. That would be best."

I nodded. I kissed Grandma and they took her

out. Shad sat down on the couch and started playing on a little tin flute. I went into the bedroom and called the convention center. It took a long time to find someone who understood what I wanted. "I have to give my mother a message. It's important." I finally got a woman who said she'd find Mom and tell her.

I went back into the living room. Shad was still sitting on the couch, blowing into the flute. He kept playing the same tune over and over. *"Yankee Doodle went to town, aridin' on his pony. . . ."*

"Don't," I said. Shad put down the flute, but a moment later he picked it up again and started all over. *"Yankee Doodle went to town. . . ."*

I went into the kitchen. I washed the dishes. I tried not to make a lot of noise. I don't know why. I didn't want to walk on the floor where Grandma had been lying. I tiptoed around the spot. It looked the same as the rest of the floor, but I couldn't put my foot on it.

I found some meat loaf and made two sandwiches. "Shad, I made you a sandwich." I put pickles on the plate and brought the sandwiches into the living room. "Sit on the rug," I said. I didn't want to mess up Grandma's couch. "What'd you do?" I asked Shad.

"Outside? I bought this flute." He took a bite of the sandwich, then a bite of pickle.

"Anything else?"

"I went into a pet store. That's where I stayed mostly." He brightened up. "You should see that place, Bunny! I'll take you there. They had little dogs in the window."

"Oh, no. Too corny."

"Six of them. They were all black. Do you think — "

"No," I said. "You know what Dad says. It wouldn't be fair to a dog to leave it at home alone all day."

"It could have the whole backyard to play in," Shad argued. He got that stubborn look on his face, which meant he was going to argue with me until I said he could have a dog.

"Shad. It's not up to me."

"You could tell Dad. He'd listen to you."

"Where do you get that idea? He wouldn't."

"He would. More than he listens to me."

Then Mom walked in. She pulled off her coat and threw it down on the couch. "What happened? Bunny, they told me — I didn't even want to take the time to call. I just came home. I got a taxi, and — did the ambulance come? Did she fall or — "

I got up and went to her. "Mom. Grandma and I were just sitting in the kitchen and talking." My throat got thick. "And, and she lit a cigarette and then — " I wanted to tell her everything, but my throat was so tight I couldn't speak. "Oh, Mom." I put my arms around her and started to cry.

Chapter 17

The next day, Mom and Dad were on the phone for a long time. Then, Mom sat on the couch with me and we had a conference.

"You know, I want to be with Grandma while she's in the hospital," Mom said. "Probably ten days. Maybe two weeks. So the question is, What about you and Shad? Here's our options. First, you and Shad could stay right here. Well, the problem with that is, what would you two do every day? Besides, I don't like you missing all that school."

I nodded. "Especially Shad." Shad is gifted. He's really smart. You would think he could miss tons of school and it would be okay. But it doesn't work that way. He gets bored and cranky when he's not in school.

"Right," Mom said. "Especially Shad. So that doesn't seem like such a great idea. You could stay on until Tuesday, when Dad will be home. Just miss a couple days of school. That's not bad. What do you think?"

I thought about staying in Toronto. And I thought about going home. And I told Mom that if Shad and I went home, it would be the best plan. "Then we don't miss any school. We can take care of ourselves for two days at home. I'll make meals and all that stuff. It wouldn't be any different if we stayed here. Because you'll be in the hospital all day, anyway."

"Yes, but I'd be here at night. You'll be home alone two nights."

"That's okay."

"You think you can handle it? You don't have to do this part, Bunny. You know you're going to have to take over for me, anyway. I'm sorry to say it, but Dad doesn't have a clue about the house. I've spoiled him."

"I can handle it, Mom."

"What about Shad? Do you think he can get along okay without me or Dad around?"

I nodded. "Mom, I'll take good care of him." I felt sort of solemn, like I was taking a vow or something. For a minute I even forgot about Grandma — that she was the reason Mom and I were having this discussion — and I felt really proud and happy.

Mom said she'd have to talk to Dad again and later that night I heard her on the phone for a long time. The next morning she drove us to the bus station.

In the bus, I let Shad have the window seat. The trip seemed really long, even with him to keep me company. I kept thinking about Grandma. Every time I closed my eyes, I would see her lying on the floor.

Mom had given me money for a taxi when we got back. I was glad. I just wanted to be home.

When I gave the taxi driver the money, he looked at it and said, "Don't break your heart." He drove off.

"Did you give him a tip?" Shad said.

"I paid him what the meter said. Fifteen dollars for a little ride home!"

"You're supposed to tip him, Bunny."

"How do you know that?" I shoved him toward the house. "Mom didn't say anything about it." I unlocked the front door and we went in. I dropped my knapsack on the floor and took off my jacket. It was late. It was dark. The house felt empty.

I hung up my jacket and turned on some lights. Shad was still standing in the hall, looking around like he didn't even recognize our house. "Will you sleep in my room tonight, Bunny?"

"No, I don't like the smell in your room."

"What smell?"

"All your little pets smell, Shad."

"Not to me."

"Well, they do to me."

He went upstairs to his room. I walked through the house. It wasn't the first time I'd ever been home without Mom and Dad. I tried to pretend it was just another evening when they were out visiting friends, but it wasn't the same thing. I don't know why, but the house even sounded emptier, as if the rooms and the walls and the furniture knew that Mom and Dad were really somewhere else, far away.

I called Emily. I told her what happened. "Oh, Bunny! Your grandmother." When I told her about the empty sound, she said, "I know. It was just like that after my father left."

Shad came down the stairs.

"You can sleep in my room, if you want to," I said. "How's the petting zoo? Are they okay? Did they drink up all the water?"

"They're pretty hungry. And I have to clean their cages."

"Well, go ahead and do it."

"You don't have to tell me. I'm hungry. We didn't have that much to eat on the bus."

"Okay, make yourself something."

"Bunny, if I'm hungry at night, Mom always makes it."

I went into the kitchen. There wasn't that much in the refrigerator. Usually, we shop on Friday night when Mom gets paid. I found a frozen pizza and put it in the oven.

Mom phoned before we went to sleep. "Everything's fine," I said. "Did you see Grandma?"

"I was at the hospital all afternoon."

We talked some more. Then she talked to Shad. Right after she hung up, Dad phoned and we both talked to him, too. Shad was on the upstairs phone, I was on the downstairs phone.

"I'm sleeping in Bunny's room, Dad," Shad said.

"Good," Dad said. "That's a really good idea."

The next morning, it was kind of fun being in the house alone. Shad and I could talk as loud as we wanted to. Usually, in the mornings, Dad is sort of grumpy. Even if we're whispering, he's always saying, "Kids, please, would you tone it down!"

Breakfast was okay and I was thinking everything was going great until Shad couldn't find his science book. We spent half an hour looking for that book all over the house. We finally found it on top of the refrigerator. "How'd it get there?" I said.

"I bet Mom put it there. Remember the time she put my milk money in the freezer?"

"Now we're both going to be late for school." We ran out of the house, then I had to dash back to lock up, which I almost forgot to do.

I never thought I was a big worrier, except about my name and my teeth. But all that day in school, I worried about a lot of things. About Grandma first. And then about all the things I'd have to do to take care of Shad and me, and would I have enough time for everything. "You will, you will," Emily kept saying. And I kept saying, "I hope so, but I don't know, Em. . . ."

On the way home, I had to buy food for supper, and then I worried that if something held Dad up in San Diego, we wouldn't have enough money to buy anything else. When I called Emily later, she said, "Bunny, your mom could cable you money overnight."

I adjusted the phone. I had it stuck between my ear and my shoulder, while I peeled carrots for supper. "How do you know all that stuff?"

"It's no big deal. It's just that my father did it for us one time when Mom was sick."

That was the second night we were in the house

alone. "Do you want to sleep in your own room?"
I asked Shad, while we were eating supper.

"Maybe."

"We better clean up the kitchen tonight." We
hadn't washed the dishes from last night or this
morning.

"We could do it tomorrow."

I was tempted. Then I thought, What if Dad
comes home early and everything's a mess? "No,
tonight," I said.

We were just loading up the sink with soapsuds
when Dad called. Shad spoke to him first, then I
did. "Hello, Dad. Where are you? Still in San
Diego?"

"Yes, this is the last day, honey. Shad sounds
good. Are you okay?"

"Uh huh. We were just cleaning up the kitchen."

"Okay. I talked to Mom earlier today. Grandma's
improving a little bit."

We talked for a while more. Then we finished
the dishes. I knew Mom was going to call, but it
was later before she did. I was just getting out of
the shower and Shad was watching tv. Mom wanted
to know everything, how we were, what we ate
for supper, if we got to school on time, and did
Shad take a shower.

"Not yet. I'll make sure he does."

"Okay, honey. Good."

I thought she was going to hang up. "Mom,
wait. What about Grandma?"

"She was more alert today. We don't know the
full story yet. They're still doing tests." She told
me more things about Grandma. That the stroke
had paralyzed her left side. That Grandma still

wasn't talking. Then Mom said the worst thing of all. "She keeps crying. The doctors told me that it's typical of stroke patients, but still. . . . You know Grandma. She was always so peppy. And now. . . ." Mom's voice trailed off.

I didn't say anything. I had this awful feeling in my chest. I didn't even want to talk to Mom anymore, and we hung up a few minutes later.

After he showered, Shad came into my room. He was wearing his bathrobe and slippers. He was carrying one of his white rats, petting it.

"Bunny? What's going to happen to Grandma?"

"I don't know."

"What did Mommy say?"

"The doctors are still finding out things." I wished he would stop asking me questions. I didn't want to talk about it. I didn't want to think about Grandma crying.

He stood there with the white rat in his palm, petting it.

"Who's that?" I said.

"This is Zelda." He put her on his head, like a hat. "Is Grandma going to die?"

I wanted to shout at him, and I couldn't. It was like being with Grandma again, in the kitchen, when she was lying on the floor, looking at me and looking at me, and I was so scared, and I couldn't say it. "She had a stroke, Shad. That's not dying."

"Are you sure?"

Of course, I wasn't sure. I opened my mouth, then I shut it. Shad looked so little to me. I don't mean he looked small or short, but like a little boy. Young.

"Mom says people recover from strokes. They get therapy and stuff."

"Oh. Okay." Shad sat down in the rocker and put Zelda on his arm and played with her, until it was time to go to bed.

Chapter 18

Grandma was in the hospital in Toronto for ten days. Mom called home almost every night. First she'd talk to Dad, then to Shad and me. Sometimes we'd all get on the phone together, Dad in his study, Shad in the kitchen, and me in Mom and Dad's bedroom. Then, for a few minutes, with all of us talking at once, telling each other things and laughing, I'd almost forget about Grandma. But at some point, every day, Mom would say, "Well, let me give you my report on Grandma." And then she'd say something like, "She's getting along." Or, "Today I saw an improvement over yesterday."

A couple of days after Grandma was discharged from the hospital, Mom drove back home with her. Even though Grandma could get the best care and therapy in Toronto, Mom didn't want to leave her there. "It would be like leaving her alone," she said. "I can't do that."

And Dad said, "Don't even discuss it, Lorraine. Just bring her here."

When I heard Grandma was coming home with Mom to live with us, I was happy. I really was. The way I thought about it was this: Grandma had been in the hospital, she'd been sick and now she was better, and just had to get really well. Which she would do with us.

I don't know what I thought about how she would look. I didn't really think about it. Didn't let myself. Maybe I just expected her to look the way she always had. Sometimes I remembered her lying on the kitchen floor with her leg tangled in the chair. Whenever that came into my mind, though, I'd quickly think of something else.

I'd think of a camping trip our family took a few years ago. How one time we stopped at a place called Crystalline Lake and Dad and I stood on the little bit of sandy shore and pitched stones into the water, just as the sun was going down. The water was like dark, rippled paper.

Saturday, Dad and I worked all day fixing up one of the downstairs rooms for Grandma. The good thing about it was that it was on the south side of the house, with three windows facing the backyard. The bad thing about it was that it was a mess and besides cleaning up, we had to take out an old red velvet couch that breathed dust and weighed a ton.

We half dragged, half carried it out. Dad was puffing. First he was cheerful and kept saying, "I ought to take up jogging again." Then he got less cheerful and kept saying, "Careful of the floors. Don't scratch them."

I vacuumed the room and Dad washed the windows. There were quite a few spider webs in the corners. When the room was clean, we took apart one of the beds in the upstairs spare room, carried it downstairs, and put it back together again.

Emily called, but I didn't even have time to talk to her. We put clean sheets and blankets on the bed. We brought in an easy chair from Dad's study, and his and Mom's tv, and a lamp.

"My arms are sore from all that lifting and carrying," I told Emily when she called in the morning.

"But how lucky that your grandmother is coming to live with you."

"I know. Wait, Emily." I had the phone clamped between my ear and shoulder again. I got the broom and swept the kitchen floor while Emily and I talked.

"When was the last time the famous grandmother came to visit you?"

"You mean, the famous Toronto Blue Jays fanatic. It was, umm, two years ago. Don't you remember? We all went to see one of those old Walt Disney pictures. *Fantasia*. That was it. Maybe we'll all do something together again," I said.

Late that day, Mom came home. It was almost seven o'clock. We were just finishing supper and wondering where Mom was, when we heard the car horn honk. Dad jumped up like a kangeroo and ran out.

Shad and I went after him. Mom got out of the car first. Dad hugged her. Then he reached into the car and brought out a folded wheelchair. For a moment, I looked at it and I thought, What is this? What's that for? Then Mom helped Grandma out of the car, and I knew that all the things I'd been thinking were wrong. All the things about going places with Grandma, and how she was just coming to live with us, and only had to recuperate from an illness.

I had never thought of Grandma as small. She wasn't a huge woman, but she was substantial. She was solid. I could hug her and lean against her and even knock into her playfully and it would be okay. Now she was different.

She looked like someone else. Someone tiny and frail. Someone almost — *disposable*. She had shrunk. A terrible joke came into my mind. *Somebody put her in the dryer and shrank her.*

I remembered how, when I read *Alice in Wonderland*, I especially liked the part where she drank from the bottle that said, DRINK ME. She did. And she got smaller and smaller and smaller. And smaller. That was how Grandma looked. Except that Alice was tiny and still looked just like herself in every detail.

But Grandma was tiny and didn't look like herself at all. She looked like a little, old person, a little tiny, frail, bent someone. A person I sort of recognized, but not really. What I recognized were her clothes. But even they looked different, like she was wearing someone else's clothes, the clothes of someone much bigger.

Dad unfolded the wheelchair, and Mom helped Grandma into it. Her left arm hung by her side. Mom put the arm in Grandma's lap. She put it in Grandma's lap like it was a *thing*. It didn't look like a real arm. It didn't look alive. It was just there, not doing anything. Compared to the rest of Grandma, it seemed big, heavy. It seemed to drag her whole side down. She was tipped over to one side, to that left side.

Shad ran up to her and kissed her, but I couldn't. I just stood in the doorway. I didn't know if I should hug her or what. "How was your trip?" I said. I could hear how polite my voice sounded, as if she were someone I was just meeting. Or someone I didn't really care about.

One side of Grandma's face was twitching. But the other side of her face didn't do anything at all. "Hello, Bunny," she said. She talked sort of slurred and stumbling. It made me feel sick.

"Grandma's tired from the trip," Mom said. "Come on, Mommy, let's get you to your room."

Dad had bought a big pot of yellow and gold daffodils. They were on the windowsill. Beautiful flowers. Just the sort of thing Grandma loved. She didn't notice them. She didn't say anything about all the work we'd done. She sat in her wheelchair, her head drooping. "I'm . . . tired," she said. "I'm . . . tired."

Mom opened Grandma's suitcase and took out a nightgown. "You guys better go." Dad and Shad went out. Mom lifted Grandma's arms to take off her dress. She undressed her like a baby. First one arm out, then the other, then the dress over her head. She had to do everything for Grandma. She put Grandma's nightgown on her, she took off Grandma's shoes, and she washed Grandma's hands and face and tucked her into bed.

"Bunny . . . darling," Grandma said, from the

bed. She lifted her good arm and held out her hand to me.

I didn't go to her. I stood in the doorway. I waved to her. "Good-night, Grandma."

Later, in my room, I shut the door and cried. I couldn't stop crying. I lay down on my bed and put the pillow over my head. After a while, I fell asleep.

In the morning, I didn't want to get out of bed. I didn't want to see Grandma the way she was now. I never wanted to see her that way.

Mom came by and knocked on the door. "Bunny? You'll be late if you don't get up right now."

I didn't move. Mom came back two more times, and finally I got up and dressed. I didn't eat breakfast, I just left the house with my books and ran all the way to school.

Chapter 19

Suddenly, everything in our house was for Grandma. Day and night, we had to be quiet because Grandma was resting, or Grandma was sleeping, or Grandma had had a difficult day. Or a hard night. Shad and I couldn't argue, couldn't disagree with each other, couldn't even raise our voices, because it might upset Grandma.

Even something like having a snack changed. You couldn't go in the refrigerator and take anything you wanted to eat, because certain foods were reserved for Grandma. "We have to coax her appetite," Mom said. She bought expensive, special tropical fruits, mangoes and papayas, and the first California strawberries.

Mom had missed two weeks of work before she came home from Toronto. She took off another week, until Grandma got rested from the trip and used to things in our house. Those three weeks were all Mom's vacation time, plus her sick days, which meant that this year our family wouldn't go anyplace together, the way we always did.

The house sounded different. Quieter. Everyone tiptoeing around. UPS delivered boxes of Grandma's things that Mom had sent from Toronto. They were piled up in the hall. And the house smelled of medicines and rubbing alcohol. It didn't seem like our house. I didn't want to go in when I came home from school. And when I did go in, I just went to my room.

Mom came into my room after supper one night. "Beginning next week, Grandma's going to therapy every day," Mom said. She rubbed the back of her neck. "I'll be driving her to the center — St. Camillus — in the mornings, and Dad will leave his office early in the afternoon and bring her home."

I sat at my desk and fidgeted with a ballpoint pen. "Okay."

"And you, Bunny," Mom said, "I want you to come home right after school every day and be in the house with Grandma, until either Dad or I come home."

"I thought you just said Dad was leaving his office early."

"Right. But he has to go back. And Grandma really shouldn't be in the house alone." Mom went to the window and pulled down the shade.

"So I have to baby-sit Grandma."

"You're not baby-sitting her," Mom said. "Where do you get that idea?"

"That's what it seems like to me." I got up and pulled the shade up again.

Mom gave me a look, but she didn't say anything else.

Every day that week, I didn't feel good. I didn't have any energy. Sometimes my head ached. It really hurt. One day I didn't eat anything all day. Emily was the only one who noticed anything.

"You're in such a bad mood," she said.

I shrugged. I didn't want to talk about it.

Friday, after school, I went home with Emily. She was talking about a letter her father wrote her. Happy talk. She couldn't stop talking about that letter. We got to her house and went into the kitchen to make a snack for the twins. "You know how many letters I've gotten from my father in my whole life?" she said. She handed me a can of apple juice to open.

"How many?" I'd stopped listening. I was thinking that this was my last weekend of freedom.

"I counted them. The first one he wrote me when I was four and he was — " She stopped. "Bunny, look what you did. You just spilled juice all over the counter."

I looked down. I'd been pouring the apple juice, and I'd missed the glasses entirely. "So what!" I said. "Don't make such a big fuss over nothing!"

"I'm not making a big fuss," Emily said. "If I hadn't said anything, you would have spilled the whole can." She got a rag and wiped it up.

I stared at her. I hated her. I thought, She's wiping up the spill just to make me feel bad, to make me feel even worse. It was a stupid thought, but it seemed true to me at the moment. I felt so bad. I felt like I'd just lived through the worst week of my life, and no one understood and no one cared.

Emily wrung out the rag. "What's the matter, Bunny?"

"Nothing. Leave me alone." I started crying.

"Who's crying?" Wilma said, from the other room.

Emily shut the kitchen door. "Bunny. . . ." She rubbed my arm. "Come on, sit down." It was so weird. It was role reversal. It was like all the times I'd rubbed her arm or her back and told her to sit down and given her a tissue and said, "Blow your nose." All the times I'd "rescued" her. And now she was rescuing me. She made me sit down, she gave me a tissue, and I blew my nose.

"Is it your grandma?" Emily said.

"It's not fair."

"Who said everything's got to be fair? I don't think it's fair that my parents got divorced, either, but they did."

"I don't want to talk about your problems! Why did it happen to Grandma? Why me? Why us? I hate it, Emily. I hate it, I hate it, I hate it." I started crying again.

Wilma came in and Emily got up. "No, Wilma. Go out. Stay out of here now."

"Why's Bunny crying? Bunny." She came and stood by me and petted my hair.

Emily gave Wilma the juice and crackers on a tray and she went back into the living room to watch tv with Chris.

"Emily. All I want to do when I'm home is stay in my room. I don't want to see Grandma. I don't want to talk to her. I can't tell Mom or Dad that!

I can't tell anybody how I feel. They would hate me if they knew."

"I don't hate you," Emily said.

"You don't count."

"Thanks a lot."

"You know what I mean. I mean my family. I wish I could leave home."

"Come live with us."

"Maybe I will." I blew my nose again.

"We'll put another bed in my room."

"A cot would be okay. I don't need much."

"It would be fun."

"I'd help you with Wilma and Chris. Your mother would hardly even know I was here."

Emily got up and started washing dishes. "I'm listening," she said. "I just have to do these."

I stared at the wall. "Grandma can't do anything anymore for herself. . . . This is the worst thing that has ever happened to me." I put my head down on my arms.

I heard the water running out of the sink. Emily sat down next to me again and put her hand on my back. "Bunny. It didn't happen to you."

I sat there for a long time with my head down on my arms. I was hearing what Emily said. *It didn't happen to you.* I didn't want to hear it, but the words kept repeating themselves in my head. *It didn't happen to you.* At first, I didn't even know what they meant. They were just words. It was like hearing something in another language. *It didn't happen to you. It didn't happen to you.* I knew I should understand, but I didn't. My head felt thick. I think I fell asleep for a moment. And I still heard those words. Then I knew what they meant.

"I've hardly even gone in to see her," I said. "Grandma's been here a whole week." I lifted my head. "Emily, I'm an awful person."

"No, you're not. If you were, you wouldn't care. You wouldn't be crying."

"You never cry, except when you're sick, and that doesn't count."

"I do," Emily said. "You just don't see me. I cry in my room and then, when I come out, I just try to smile, because . . . you know. Here, drink this juice."

I drank the juice. I ate some toast. Then I ate a cupcake. I felt suddenly so hungry, as if I hadn't eaten for a week. I opened a box of crackers and buttered a whole bunch and ate them, with another glass of juice. "Do you really cry in your room, Emily?"

She nodded.

"I don't like that. I don't like that you cry alone. You're my friend and if you're crying, I don't want you to cry alone."

"Bunny, suppose it's eleven o'clock at night. I'm in my house. You're in your house. I feel sad. I feel like crying. What am I supposed to do?"

"Call me up. Send me a telegram. Say, CRYING. NEED HELP IMMEDIATELY. Then I'll cry, too. We'll be crying together."

As soon as I got home, I went into Grandma's room. She was lying on the bed, covered with a blanket. I stood in the doorway. She looked at me with big, big eyes. The stroke had made everything about her smaller, except her eyes. There were tears leaking out of them.

"Why are you crying?" It wasn't what I meant to say. Or the way I meant to say it. It came out hard and rough. I thought she was crying because she knew all the mean and terrible things that had been in my head.

The tears kept coming out of her eyes.

I wanted to scream or howl or hit my head against the wall. I went to the window and looked out at our backyard. "Did you see the trees, Grandma? They're all getting green." I didn't know what I was saying. Just talking. "Shad wants to build bigger cages for his animals. I think if Mom would let him, he'd give them a whole room to themselves."

"He's sweet," she said.

"Yes." After a moment: "I'm not."

"My Bunny," she said.

I leaned my head against the glass. I was remembering how unhappy my name had made me, how terrible I thought it was to have big front teeth and be taller than anybody. Oh, Bunny, I thought, now you would be happy if you could see Grandma the way she used to be.

After a while, I sat down on the bed.

Those tears. They kept leaking out of her eyes.

I tried to think of a joke. Something funny. "Grandma, there's a slogan the Swiss have. Every little bit Alps."

"What?"

She didn't get it. I tried again. "I saw a sign over a dairy today, Grandma. YOU CAN'T BEAT OUR MILK. BUT YOU CAN WHIP OUR CREAM.

"Eh?"

I began to feel desperate. I wanted those tears

to stop. "Listen, Grandma, I heard that the Jays are three games down." I sat close to her and talked right to her. "Now my theory is that you stopped rooting for them. Grandma, you just can't do that. You know how it is, you root for them and they win. You lie down on the job, and they lose. My idea is that you and I better start spending a little time every day concentrating on the Jays."

She nodded.

I jumped up and pranced like a cheerleader. "Blue Jays! Blue Jays!" I threw out my arms. Sank to my knees. "We love ya, Blue Jays!"

One side of Grandma's face lifted. A smile, I think. I picked up her hand and kissed it.

Chapter 20

Every day, now, Grandma goes to therapy. I come home directly after school, usually a few minutes before Dad comes back with Grandma. As soon as I hear our car, I go outside.

"Go back to work, dear," Grandma says to Dad, in her new slow voice. "Bunny's here." Everything she does is very slow. She doesn't need the wheelchair anymore. She has a cane now, but I carry it, and she holds my arm as we go into the house.

"Grandma, do you want some juice or something?"

"I'm tired. I'll rest first." She leans on her cane. Her left leg drags. We go into her room. "You could just pull the shades, darling." I cover her with a blanket.

Sometimes, she's not so tired. She comes into the kitchen and talks to me and Shad. She likes to sit in a chair by the window, looking out. Sometimes she's very quiet, you don't hear anything, but when you look over at her, you see tears running down her cheeks.

It's better when she does her exercises. She sits at the table and, with her good right hand, she lifts her left arm and puts it on the table in front of her. She still moves her left arm as if it's a thing. Then, with her right hand, she moves each separate finger of her left hand back and forth twenty times. She's working up to fifty. And she tries to make a fist.

Star came home for one weekend to see Grandma. Everybody made a big fuss over her. Me, too. I was so glad to see her I forgot to be mad at her. But I was mad again by the time she went back to school, because all the time she could spare for me was five minutes. Excuse me. I mean four minutes and twelve seconds. I timed it. She poked her head in my room Saturday night. "So, how's it going, Bunny?"

I decided to be just as cool as she was. "Oh, fine."

"So, okay," she said.

"Okay what?"

"Just — okay." She smiled.

I hate to say it, she has a beautiful smile. She has teeth just like me, but on her they don't look funny at all. When she smiled, I almost decided I would never be mad at her again, no matter what. "What about you, Star?"

"What about me?"

"All those phone calls to Mom — "

"Oh, that." She waved her hand. "Nothing."

That was it. That was my big conversation with my sister, Star. She went back to school Sunday night.

"Look, Bunny." Grandma had just come home from therapy. She sat down at the kitchen table and without any help from her good hand, she moved her left thumb back and forth.

"Grandma! Do it again."

She did it again.

I sat down next to her and we both watched as she wriggled her thumb.

"Give you another week," I said, "and you'll be hand-wrestling me." And then I burst into tears.

"Well, Bunny," she said.

"No . . . I'm sorry . . . don't mind me."

"My little Bunny."

I tried to laugh at the idea of me being little Bunny. But, instead, I leaned against Grandma, as if she were well and strong again. "Grandma, I love you. I love you so much."

She stroked my hair with her good hand.

"How's your grandma doing?" Emily said. It was Saturday and we were in the mall shopping.

"Better. Don't you want to come over and see her?"

"Is it okay?"

"Naturally, it's okay. She'd like to see you."

"I'll come over next week on Thursday, when the twins take swimming. Do you have to get home early today?"

"Do you?"

"No. Mom's with the twins."

"Good. Me, either. Mom's with Grandma. She said take my time and have fun."

Emily linked her arm with mine. "Want to go to a movie?"

"Sure. But let's go buy my sneakers first." We walked over to The Sport Shop. I tried on three different pairs of sneakers before I found what I wanted. Then I decided to buy socks, and that took a little longer.

"Well, we better hurry," Emily said, "if we're going to the movie."

"We can always go to the next show." We got in line to pay.

"Hello, Emily," somebody said behind me. I turned around, and so did Emily. It was James. He was holding a tennis racket and a can of balls. He looked just the same, maybe better.

"James!" It was so strange seeing him. It was a whole mix-up of feelings. Right off, I got that sweaty-behind-the-knees feeling, and my face flushed hot. But, at the same time, my head didn't feel as goofy and swimmy as it had other times with him. It was more like I was seeing an old friend, someone I'd known quite a long time ago and had really liked. It made me want to hug him. But I just said, "Gosh, you run into people in the funniest places." And then I saw that I felt older in some way, as if I'd known him when I was much younger. And I hoped he would notice that I was different.

"So, what have you been up to?" he said. "Been to any more concerts?"

"No, I've been pretty busy."

"Me, too. Getting ready for graduation."

All this time, Emily had been giving James the

Big Stare. Now she was seeing for herself how good-looking he was. I gave her a little shove with my elbow. Just meaning, *See! Didn't I tell you!*

Then James said to her, "Hi, I'm James."

"Oh, excuse me, I should introduce you," I said. "James, this is — " I stopped dead. I'd never had a clue to handling this problem I'd created of the two of us having the same name — and I still didn't.

But Emily did. She stuck out her hand to James. "Hi," she said. "I'm Bunny."

I stared at her. Shy little Emily! She didn't crack a smile.

"Are you the James that Emily met at the concert?" she said.

"Yeah, I'm that James. And you're Bunny?"

"Right. Emily's best friend," Emily said. She gave me a little smile. "Aren't I, Emily?"

"Yes," I said. "Best friends."

We stood around and talked for a few minutes. I think I was almost going to be jealous, because James talked as much to Emily as he did to me. But I was too distracted by the goofiness of hearing him calling Emily Bunny. Besides, he kept looking at me, and once he reached out and touched my arm as he was saying something.

"Next, please," the boy at the cash register said. I put my stuff down on the counter. Then James went through and we all walked out together. We stood outside the store.

"We should get going if we want to see that movie," Emily said.

I looked at James. "Well . . . 'bye."

He gave my hand a squeeze. " 'Bye, Emily. It was great seeing you. I know we're going to run into each other again." He ruffled my hair. Right then, I decided that if I ever did see him again, I'd tell him the truth about my name. Only not now. It was too complicated.

We walked away. Then he came running after us. I heard him and turned around. I thought he was going to kiss me or something. Instead, he put his hand on Emily's shoulder and said, "I'll remember that name, Bunny."

I thought, Why did he say that? And then he did kiss me. A quick kiss on the cheek. Before I could think, I kissed him back on his cheek. Then he put his hands on my shoulders and kissed me on the other cheek. And I kissed him on his other cheek. And — well, that was it. I could have stayed there, cheek kissing, but it didn't work out that way. He said 'bye again and I said 'bye, and he went in one direction and Emily and I went in the other.

We missed the beginning of the first show. "Let's come back. We can go get something to eat now," Emily said.

"Sure, *Bunny*," I said.

"Oh, *Emily*," she said. We started laughing and calling each other by the other's name. We got really silly.

"Do you think he guessed anything?" Emily said.

"I don't think so." I looked at her. "He liked you."

Emily's face got red. "He liked my name. I mean,

your name. Bunny, I wish you could have seen your face when I said, 'Hi! I'm Bunny.' "

That started us off again. When we finally calmed down, we linked arms and went off to have some gelato.

About the Author

NORMA FOX MAZER is the author of more than twenty books for young readers, among them the Newbery honor winner *After the Rain*, as well as *Taking Terri Mueller*, *When We First Met*, and *Downtown*. Ms. Mazer has twice won the Lewis Carroll Shelf Award; she has also won the California Young Reader Medal and has been nominated for the National Book Award.

B, My Name Is Bunny is a companion book to *A, My Name Is Ami*; *C, My Name Is Cal*; *D, My Name Is Danita*; and *E, My Name Is Emily* (which is also a sequel to *B, My Name Is Bunny*), all published by Scholastic.

Ms. Mazer lives with her husband, author Harry Mazer, in the Pompey Hills outside Syracuse, New York.